MAKING OUT

Prom Night

MAKING OUT

Megan Stine

BERKLEY JAM BOOKS, NEW YORK

A Parachute Press Book

THE BERKLEY PUBLISHING GROUP
Published by the Penguin Group
Penguin Group (USA) Inc.
375 Hudson Street, New York, New York 10014, USA
Penguin Group (Canada), 90 Eglinton Avenue East, Suite 700, Toronto, Ontario M4P 2Y3, Canada
(a division of Pearson Penguin Canada Inc.)
Penguin Books Ltd., 80 Strand, London WC2R 0RL, England
Penguin Group Ireland, 25 St. Stephen's Green, Dublin 2, Ireland (a division of Penguin Books Ltd.)
Penguin Group (Australia), 250 Camberwell Road, Camberwell, Victoria 3124, Australia
(a division of Pearson Australia Group Pty. Ltd.)
Penguin Books India Pvt. Ltd., 11 Community Centre, Panchsheel Park, New Delhi—110 017, India
Penguin Group (NZ), Cnr. Airborne and Rosedale Roads, Albany, Auckland 1310, New Zealand
(a division of Pearson New Zealand Ltd.)
Penguin Books (South Africa) (Pty.) Ltd., 24 Sturdee Avenue, Rosebank, Johannesburg 2196,
South Africa

Penguin Books Ltd., Registered Offices: 80 Strand, London WC2R 0RL, England

This book is an original publication of The Berkley Publishing Group.

Teenage couples at prom photograph by Tony Anderson/FPG/Getty Images.
Cover design by Monica Benalcazar.
Text design by Tiffany Estreicher.

PRINTING HISTORY
Berkley JAM trade paperback edition / October 2006

Library of Congress Cataloging-in-Publication Data

Stine, Megan.
Prom night : making out / Megan Stine.—Berkley JAM trade paperback ed.
p. cm.
Summary: Prom night finds high school student Lisa Marie juggling too many boys and her two girlfriends each hiding a secret.
ISBN 0-425-21179-7
[1. Proms—Fiction. 2. Interpersonal relations—Fiction. 3. Washington (D.C.)—Fiction.] I. Title.
PZ7.S86035Pr 2006
[Fic]—dc22

2006008525

PRINTED IN THE UNITED STATES OF AMERICA

10 9 8 7 6 5 4 3 2 1

Chapter 1

"Try it on."

Lisa Marie Santos stared at the size six Maxazria dress. She fingered the lace edge detail around the neck and felt her heart beating faster. It was the most beautiful dress she'd ever seen in her life: black peau de soi silk deliberately crinkled and cut on the bias, with tight princess seams and a ragged, irregular hemline trimmed in the tiniest pale pink pearls and lace edging.

A cross between boho and classic Audrey Hepburn.

This is the one, Lisa Marie thought. The dress that would make her senior prom night everything it was supposed to be. The one that would make her feel like a princess and look every bit as drop-dead gorgeous as her older sister had looked three years ago when she was Homecoming Queen. There was only one problem.

"It's five hundred dollars," she said, trying not to sound like that was way out of her league. Just out of her price range.

"Is there any chance your parents will change their minds?" Heather Proule asked.

Lisa Marie's two best friends—Heather Proule and Marianna Kazanjian—fidgeted uncomfortably. She knew they were trying to figure out what to say—they had been listening to her complain all afternoon about the budget her parents had given her. One hundred dollars for a dress, shoes, bag, and hairstyle. It was ridiculous. And totally unfair. Her sister Angela had been given free rein for everything when she was in high school.

But that was three years ago, before Angela's college tuition kicked in. Now the whole family was on a budget.

Bye-bye trips back home to the Isla de Margarita off the Venezuelan coast. Hello neighborhood pool.

"They won't," Lisa Marie said. "Money is seriously tight. My mom hasn't even had her hair colored in three months."

"Well, maybe it's too early to shop," Marianna said. "Prom is still seven weeks away. Maybe the price will come down."

"Too early to shop?" Lisa Marie pretended to be shocked. "Are you feeling okay? Take her temperature, Heather."

"No, we should check her DNA," Heather joked. "She must be some sort of bio-copy of the real Marianna."

"Ha! Like I don't know how to shop? I'm more hard-core than either of you," Marianna argued. "Remember last year? When Nordstrom's stayed open till eleven and they had to escort me out to my car?"

Lisa Marie laughed. "Yeah, that was good. I think they have your photo posted on the wall in the office or something."

"And the best part was, you didn't even buy anything! You were there for, what? Twelve hours? And went home empty-handed." Heather laughed. "I'll bet they loved that."

"It wasn't a good day," Marianna admitted.

"Look, all we're saying is we could keep looking for prom dresses." Heather put a sympathetic hand on Lisa Marie's arm. "Maybe you'll find something cheaper that's just as good."

Reluctantly, Lisa Marie let go of the black silk dress and continued prowling through racks of potential gowns. She and her friends had already been in nearly every chic store in Georgetown, the upscale shopping district and charming old residential section of Washington, D.C. For the past three hours, she'd been searching for the perfect thing to wear to the biggest night of her life.

Now they were back in BCBG in a mall closer to school, fingering price tags, checking sizes, and kicking into desperation mode.

Lisa Marie circled back around to the five hundred dollar dress and touched it again. She hadn't wanted anything this badly since she craved a Disco Barbie in third grade.

"Besides, we don't even have dates yet," Marianna said. "And the prom is a long way off."

"*We* don't have dates. *She* does," Heather corrected Marianna, pulling an interesting beaded green flapper-style dress off the rack.

"Like I could forget," Marianna said.

Lisa Marie glanced up. Uh-oh. Was that a tinge of jealousy in Marianna's voice? She hated for her friends to be jealous of the fact that she'd been going out with one guy, Todd Ku, for two years, while they had barely had dates.

There was no reason in the world for them to envy her, Lisa Marie thought. They were both smart, beautiful, and fun to be with—a "gag me" cliché, but it was true. They just hadn't gotten lucky yet in the guy department.

Not that Lisa Marie had exactly gotten lucky herself. Not with Todd. Marianna and Heather knew it, too.

Todd was perfect—exceptional, even. Perfectly nice, and exceptionally boring. Who wanted to date someone whose main claim to fame was being captain of the chess team?

Todd's only a habit, Lisa Marie thought. *Definitely not the love of my life.*

She wasn't even sure how she had wound up with him, except that he was the son of the first friends her parents made when they moved to D.C. from Venezuela five years ago. For some unimaginable reason, both sets of parents clearly thought their kids should go out.

In fact, she had been thinking about dumping him, but

that would be breaking Rule #1: Never dump your boyfriend right before the prom.

No, better to hang on to him until after graduation, then reassess.

"You'll both have dates for the prom, don't worry," Lisa Marie reassured her friends. "It's still way early."

In her heart, Lisa Marie knew that, in Marianna's case, even that was wishful thinking. Marianna wasn't even *allowed* to date. How was she going to hook up with someone in time for the prom?

"I think you should at least try it on," Heather said, sounding rational. "If it looks like crap on you, then you won't be disappointed. If it looks great, you can always get a job and save up for it."

Good plan. Clutching the dress like she never wanted to let go, Lisa Marie slipped into the dressing room. Why did people just leave their reject clothes lying all over the floor in American stores? After five years here, she still couldn't get used to that.

She peeled off her clothes, dropped her bra straps, and pulled the strapless dress up over her boobs. Her thick auburn hair skimmed her shoulders, framing her dark brown eyes and sensuously full lips. She looked like a darker version of Jessica Simpson, with a little bit of JLo thrown in. The dress was the perfect length—it made her legs look longer than they really were.

"Come out. Show us," Heather demanded from outside the dressing room.

Lisa Marie stepped out and twirled.

"Wow." Marianna and Heather both looked awestruck.

"So . . . you'll get a job," Heather said. "Save up. But you've got to take the dress off sometime if you want to go job hunting."

"Maybe they'd hire me to model it here?" Lisa Marie fantasized.

Heather rolled her eyes and headed back toward the display area of the store. "I'm trying on the green one."

By the time they left the store and wandered back into the shopping mall, Lisa Marie had spotted an incredible pair of Jimmy Choo shoes, decided on earrings, and was debating between two tiny evening bags—a black silk clutch with a carved rose clasp, or a teeny pink beaded bag. Now was not the time to listen to the quiet voice in the way back of her head that whispered, *Use your sister's bag and save a hundred bucks*. If it came to that, fine. But she didn't want to cave so soon.

"I need a job. Immediately," Lisa Marie announced.

"Food court?" Marianna suggested.

Lisa Marie made a face. If necessary, sure. She'd do whatever it took. But she was hoping to avoid anything involving ugly uniforms and going home with her clothes reeking of grease.

"There!" Heather pointed to a Help Wanted sign in a tuxedo rental shop.

How ironic could things get? Lisa Marie wondered. Was she really supposed to work in a formal wear shop, renting out tuxes to high school boys, so she could earn the money for her prom dress?

"Too bad you aren't a guy—maybe they'd give you a discount," Heather joked.

Lisa Marie squinted at the sign. "Look. It says, 'Retail Experience Required.'" She kept walking, scanning the windows of stores on the right and left. Then she caught the scent of the only thing in America that invariably made her feel like she was back home: coffee. There was a Starbucks straight ahead—not just a stupid middle-of-the-mall-oasis-among-the-hoards-of-shoppers Starbucks, either. It was a real Starbucks, with tables and leather furniture and a fireplace. And they had a Barista Wanted sign in the window.

"Perfect!" Marianna smiled. "You're the coffee queen—they'll have to give you the job."

It was true. When it came to roasts, grinds, espressos, macchiatos, lattes, even the best growing temperature for coffee beans, Lisa Marie was an expert. Her uncle in Cuidad Bolivar was part owner of a coffee plantation. She'd grown up with the smell of roasting coffee in her blood.

"Wait here," she told her friends, marching into the Starbucks.

Luckily, the place was slow, and the assistant manager, a guy name Gary, with outdated spiky bleached hair and a thin leather necklace around his neck, was in the mood to get the interview over with quickly.

"So why are you interested in Starbucks?" he asked.

The first part of the answer was easy. "I love the smell of coffee," she said.

Gary just stared, waiting for something more.

"And I love the idea of working for a Fortune 500 company, with opportunities to serve people in an environment where they're basically at ease and enjoying themselves," she added, layering on the bullshit.

Gary smiled.

Thank you, Angela, Lisa Marie thought, breathing a sigh of relief. Her sister had e-mailed her an article on what to say during a job interview just last week. When it came, Lisa Marie had almost deleted it. Now she was grateful for the help.

"You sound like you know what you're doing," Gary said after she went on to describe Starbucks' French roast as a blunt, smoky blend with intense richness and robust caramel flavor. "I'll try you out if you can start this afternoon."

"Seriously?" Lisa Marie's face lit up, but then she almost choked when he told her how much he could pay.

"But you get tips," Gary explained. He eyed her tight striped knit top and slim jeans. "You'll do okay. Be back here at five, and I'll have Graham train you."

Gary was definitely a little too interested in her outfit. But at least it was a job.

Quickly, she did some math in her head. Yeah, she'd be able to buy the dress *and* a pair of shoes, if she worked fifteen hours a week and got lucky with the tip jar.

"Thanks," Lisa Marie beamed.

"Starbucks partners say 'thank you'—not thanks," Gary corrected her.

Partners? What was this—a square dance?

The cell phone in her bag started ringing. Gary frowned. "And make sure that's off when you come to work."

"Sure. Thanks again. I mean *thank you*!" Lisa Marie hurried out to the mall to take her phone call.

It was Todd.

"Can you meet me in half an hour?" Todd asked.

"What's up?" Lisa Marie asked.

"Just some stuff I want to talk about," he said in his usual unemotional way.

Fine. Whatever. Though . . . it was a little odd for him to be calling and wanting to talk all of a sudden on a Saturday afternoon. They were supposed to study together the next day.

She debated whether to tell him about her new job, but Marianna and Heather were waiting.

"See you at Smooth Moves in half an hour," she said, naming her favorite smoothie place and smiling privately, happy that she'd be working someplace much cooler than that.

"Did you get the job?" Marianna asked as Lisa Marie clicked her phone closed.

"I did!"

"Coffee queen," Heather said proudly.

Lisa Marie beamed at her friends. She wondered if Todd would be as happy for her as they were—or whether he'd be pissed because her job would cut into their time together.

"I start later today. But I've got to meet Todd, so . . ."

"You have to work on a Saturday night?" Marianna sounded appalled.

Yeah. Angela never worked a Saturday night in her life. Oh, well. That was then, this was now. No point in turning the whole sibling rivalry thing into a major drama. She was tired of whining about how Angela got all the perks in the family, anyway. It felt better to actually do something about it.

"Call when you get off work," Heather said. "Maybe you can come over and watch a late movie with us."

Todd looked different when he found her sitting on their favorite bench at the edge of the food court. What was it . . . his hair? Shorter? Longer, maybe? No—he had untucked his T-shirt and was letting it hang out below his polo shirt for the first time ever. It didn't exactly look stylish on him like it did on most guys. More like sloppy. Or maybe like he just took a whiz and forgot to tuck in. But she appreciated that he was trying harder to loosen up and change his geek-with-a-pocket-protector image.

"Let's get a pretzel and share it," Lisa Marie said, suddenly famished from the shopping marathon.

Without a word of discussion, Todd went off to buy the smoothies and pretzel while Lisa Marie got the straws and napkins. Then she found a table and sat down to hold their place.

God, we're like an old married couple, Lisa Marie thought. *Without the sex.* She and Todd fooled around plenty, but she wasn't about to go all the way with someone she didn't really have strong feelings for. Even their make-out sessions were getting pretty boring these days.

But on the other hand, he was really nice to her. Always offering to do things, like install firewall software and defragment her hard drive.

Just what a girl wants.

It's the thought that counts, Lisa Marie reminded herself.

"So guess what?" she said when he had broken the pretzel in half and let her choose the piece she wanted. "I got a job."

"You did? How come?"

Should I tell him about the dress? she wondered. Or was this sort of like a wedding dress? Bad luck for him to know about it in advance? Oh, what the hell. She'd have to explain to him sometime why she wouldn't be able to hang out as much for the next few weeks.

"We went shopping for prom dresses, and I found the most amazing—"

"That's what I wanted to talk to you about," Todd interrupted.

"What?"

"Prom. I mean, not just prom, but . . ."

He wasn't looking at her. He just kept stirring his smoothie around and around.

Don't tell me he doesn't want to go to the prom, Lisa Marie thought. Not that she'd be surprised if he was freaked about the expense. Something she'd read online the other day said that with the tux, corsage, limo, dinner, prom tickets, photographs, and maybe splitting a hotel suite for the after-party, guys regularly spent close to a thousand dollars on prom night.

So what was it? Maybe he needed to forget the limo?

"Just say it," Lisa Marie said.

Todd let go of his straw and met her eyes. "I think I want to try dating other people."

Lisa Marie couldn't quite process that information. Did he mean *now*? Before the prom? Take a break from her, and then get back together in time for the prom?

Or did he mean . . . was he . . . actually . . . breaking up with her?

It was so out of left field!

Or as Todd always said when he was spouting high-level math concepts, "We've crossed the line into chaos theory."

"Why?"

"I just . . . do." Mr. Mathematical Mind. He wasn't going to try to soften it for her. He was too logical for that.

"But . . ." Lisa Marie felt her face getting hot and her throat closing up. *I am not going to cry in the food court,* she silently swore to herself. She pressed a finger into the corner of one eye, but it didn't help. Tears slipped down both cheeks.

Her head swirled with a million emotions. How could he just dump her like that? And in a public place. *That* part was unforgivable and totally humiliating. For an instant, she wondered who was watching and glanced around at the clusters of weary shoppers. But the scene was a blur—her eyes were full of tears.

"Don't cry," Todd said softly, as if he still cared about her.

"Bullshit." Lisa Marie stood up and pushed away from the table. She wasn't going to sit there and listen to him try to make her feel better about it. He was dumping her. It hurt.

She walked away, trying to choke back the feelings of rejection, trying to put this whole thing in perspective. Okay, sure—she was tired of him, and she'd been planning to dump him after graduation. But it still hurt to be the dumpee.

He hadn't even given her a hint. Not a clue.

Damn! I wish I'd dumped him first, Lisa Marie thought bitterly.

And what about the prom? What about the dress? What about working her ass off for seven weeks so she'd look like a princess? Was she really supposed to give up her Saturday nights to buy a ridiculously overpriced dress when she didn't even have a date?

Princesses don't say "ass," she thought, as she rubbed a scratchy napkin over her nose, dabbed her puffy eyes, and made her way to Starbucks.

Forget Todd. I'm going to buy that dress. I'm going to go to the prom. And I'm going to look like a princess when I do it. Period.

Chapter 2

"Sorry I can't stay to watch. Early business meeting." Marianna's father steered his Lexus SUV into the deserted parking lot behind the St. Claire's Academy athletic field and flicked off the headlights. Through the early morning fog, Marianna could see the small group of her teammates on the cross-country team warming up and stretching, getting ready for their interval training.

Her eyes immediately settled on Luke Perchik, the cutest guy on the team.

"Not a problem." Marianna tried not to let her relief show in her voice. Was her dad actually going to leave her alone during practice for a change? That would be a first. Usually he hung around being obnoxious, acting like he was some kind of an expert, giving Coach Robinson pointers on running style.

"Are you doing fartlek today?" her dad asked. "Robinson doesn't emphasize that enough, if you ask me."

Fartlek was a training regimen that Marianna especially liked—running fast, then slow, changing pace with quick bursts of speed. But having her dad push about it took all the fun away.

"I've gotta go, Dad." She jumped out of the car.

"Marianna, tell Robinson to make sure those boys aren't staring at your chest when you run," her father called out the window.

God. Her eyes darted toward the team, hoping they hadn't overheard. No one seemed to be paying any attention. *Par for the course,* she thought, wishing that Luke would at least look up to acknowledge her once in a while. She'd had a crush on him all year, but he didn't seem to notice.

But then again, why should he? When she was around him, she barely made eye contact. She didn't dare—not with her father hovering over her every second like he was Secret Service or something.

She jogged off toward the locker room to change out of her sweats and baggy T-shirt (her father-approved training uniform) and into a pair of short shorts and a tank top that let her midriff show.

By now, she was so used to maneuvering around her father's strict rules and oppressive control of her life, she didn't even think twice about it. She had all the strategies down pat: (1) take a change of clothes to school; (2) never discuss boys at the dinner table (her father could ruin any meal with his endless lectures about how all guys wanted was to get in your pants); (3) never discuss guys in her e-mails (which her father was obviously reading while she was at school); (4) pretend to be grossed out by any music video with raunchy lyrics, revealing outfits, or sexy dancing (which her father termed "borderline obscene"); and (5) behave at all times like the phrase *nice Armenian girl* didn't make her want to gag.

Translation: Act like she planned to stay a virgin for the rest of her life.

Highly likely, Marianna thought, given that she could barely even get a date. Not that she'd be allowed to go out if anyone ever asked her.

She tied her thick, black, wavy hair into a messy bun on top of her head and glanced at her reflection in the scratched locker-room mirror. Even without makeup, she had to admit that her friends were right: she looked pretty good. Her skin was flawless, and her almond eyes had a dark intensity that made total strangers stare at her.

But what was the point in looking fabulous when not one single guy at St. Claire's Academy had ever asked her out? Not unless you counted Bennie Berger, who had begged her for three solid weeks to go to Homecoming their freshmen year.

Heather and Lisa Marie claimed that guys were afraid to ask her out because she was so gorgeous. They were sure she'd turn them down.

Yeah, right. Bennie Berger was living proof of that.

She jogged back onto the field and flopped down on the damp grass to stretch her hamstrings. The ground was cold. She was going to have a big wet spot on her butt when she stood up.

"Bend it, Kazanjian," Brad Morganthal teased, jogging past her and purposely kicking her shoe.

"Just try to keep up with me," Marianna teased back. Morganthal had been running in last place on the team for several weeks.

"What do I get if I do?" Morganthal called over his shoulder, but he didn't wait for an answer.

Is he flirting with me? Marianna wondered. She glanced over at Jennifer Giles, the only other girl with any talent on the cross-country team.

"Go for it," Jennifer said. "I don't care. Brad and I broke up months ago."

Marianna blinked, surprised. "I didn't even know you were going out," she said truthfully.

Jennifer shrugged and started to say something, but Coach Robinson called her away.

"So what was your time on Friday?" a voice right behind Marianna asked.

Still leaning forward, reaching for her toes, Marianna twisted her head around to see who was asking.

Luke's soft blondish-brown hair flopped over his sky blue sweatband. He grinned at her as he bent and twisted, loosening up.

Was he actually talking to her? She couldn't quite believe it.

Too quickly, she sat up and stammered, "My time? I ran 29:14, but I didn't do tempo training last week, so I think I can improve."

"I doubt it," Luke said.

"Why?" Marianna's heart folded in half. Luke Perchik, the love of her life, was finally talking to her . . . just to dis her?

"Because you're already running about ten times better than anyone else on the team," he said.

He bent at the waist, hands on his hips, and swiveled back and forth, shooting her a grin each time he turned in her direction.

"Thanks." Marianna pretended to stretch again, although she was more interested in making sure her hair didn't fall the wrong way and her tank top didn't bunch up, making her look fat. Her pulse started racing. There had to be some way to keep this conversation going . . .

Say something, Marianna, she told herself. *Anything*. Her brain went blank.

"So, uh, what time did Coach say to meet at Warburton on Saturday?" she asked.

So lame.

"Ten, I think." Luke answered like he wasn't sure himself. Then he squatted beside her. "Listen . . ." His tone sounded half worried, half nervous. "I was thinking . . ."

Just then, Coach blew his whistle. "Move it, Perchik!" Robinson called. "I want to see your stride before you hit the road."

"You were thinking?" Marianna prompted him, wishing he'd finish his sentence. She had the vague feeling that he was trying to ask her out. Wishful thinking, no doubt.

"You, too, Kazanjian!" Coach shouted.

Luke ran off without answering. In the distance, she could see him taking a lap around the track before he hit the trail that led into the woods. She thought about following him, trying to catch up, but she didn't want to be too obvious.

She took a lap to warm up, then Coach Robinson called her over to give her a few pointers about her stride. Finally he let her go, and she pounded toward the trail, entering the woods right behind Jennifer Giles.

The trees were bare except for the evergreens. A few young buds poked out of some maple tree branches. Still, the woods were darker than the field, and quiet. Marianna loved the feeling she had when she was running in there: free and alone.

"Hey—hold up!"

Her head jerked around, but her training was deeply ingrained: never stop running. Luke was behind her, trying to catch up. Apparently he'd been waiting in a clump of pine trees just off the trail. With his powerful, long stride, he was even with her a few moments later. They jogged along side by side for a minute, and she sneaked a look at his sweaty chest.

Luke was the definition of *hot*. He was the right height, too. At five foot ten, Marianna was taller than a lot of senior guys, but Luke towered over her.

"Hi," she panted, her voice jerky as her feet hit the earth.

"Hi. You're hard to catch, you know that?"

"I've never seen you trying," she said cautiously, in an effort to sound just a little bit flirty, but not too much, in case she'd misunderstood.

"Listen," he said, his voice pounding, too. "I've been wanting to ask you. Do you, uh . . . maybe . . . want to go out sometime?"

"Sure!" She blurted out her answer without thinking, her face bright from both pleasure and the heat of the run.

"Great. How about a movie on Friday?" Luke asked. "They're showing the 1970s version of *King Kong* at the Retro Metro. I thought it would be a kick."

"Definitely." The minute she said yes, her stomach formed a knot. How was she going to get away with this? It was one thing to tell her dad she was studying with Heather on a Tuesday night, and then she and her friends would all sneak out to go shopping.

But a real date? Luke might expect to come over, meet her parents, pick her up. What were the chances that her dad would be okay with any of that?

"Excellent. Okay, I've gotta make time, or Robinson will axe me," he said, powering forward. He sprinted ahead of her, waving over his shoulder. "I'll, um, talk to you." Then he turned down a path that was a shortcut through the woods, and was gone.

Oh, man. Marianna was so pumped, she could barely keep herself from sprinting through the woods, leaping over fallen branches, darting past Jennifer Giles and two of the other fastest people on the team. So what if self-restraint was one of Coach Robinson's five favorite "Power Words for Winners"? She didn't want to restrain herself right now. She was going on a date!

Somehow.

"So what *exactly* did you do to get his attention?" Lisa Marie asked at lunch, when Marianna had told her friends what happened. "I need pointers here. I'm single again, remember?"

"Nothing. That's the problem. I have no idea what I did, so I'll never be able to tell you. But if this doesn't work out with Luke, I swear I'll be dateless for the next ten years."

"Don't be ridiculous," Heather said. "Any guy would be crazy not to want to go out with you."

"It's fabulous," Lisa Marie said. "I *told* you you'd have a date for the prom!"

"Do you think?" Marianna didn't want to get ahead of herself, but that's what she'd been secretly fantasizing about all day.

What if Luke asked her to the prom? It would be amazing, perfect, wonderful.

But what if her dad wouldn't let her go?

"I'll bet he's going to ask you," Lisa Marie predicted. "I mean, look at it this way. It's prom season. Guys start to get fidgety. A lot of them are lining up dates already."

"Yeah, but Luke and I haven't even gone out *once* yet," Marianna worried out loud. "He might not be into me after he gets to know me."

"Not a possibility," Heather said.

"Well, even if he asks me, you know my dad. I'm lucky if he lets me out of the house to take out the trash! How am I going to talk him into letting me go to the prom at all—let alone with a guy?"

"I know, I know," Lisa Marie agreed. She chewed her finger. "You're right, we've got prom issues. Plus Heather and I have no prospects. I'm seriously freaked about being single right now."

"We could say we're all going to the prom together," Heather suggested tentatively. "The three of us. Your dad would be okay with that, wouldn't he? And if none of us gets dates, we can actually do it."

Marianna wasn't sure her dad would buy it, but it sounded like the best shot she had.

"That's perfect," Lisa Marie chimed in, clearly relieved she didn't have to stress quite as much over not having a date.

"Yeah," Marianna agreed. "That might work. Maybe I can tell my dad that prom has changed, and now it's a girls-only event. Do you think he'd buy that?"

Lisa Marie laughed. "Tell him it's a community service event. Just say we're dressing up and going to a nursing home to read to the elderly and cheer them up."

"Yeah, and you're getting a Girl Scout badge for it," Heather added. "The prom badge."

Marianna tried to laugh, but nothing about her dad was too funny.

Besides, Luke hadn't even asked her to the prom yet. And maybe he wouldn't.

Definitely he wouldn't—unless she could figure out a way to talk her Neanderthal dad into letting her go on one single date.

Just one.

By Friday.

Chapter 3

My best friends are nothing like me, Heather thought with a pang, getting up to clear her lunch tray a few minutes early. She'd been listening to Marianna and Lisa Marie ramble on about trying to snag dates for the prom for the last twenty-two minutes, and the strain was killing her.

How long could she go on pretending to be interested in dating guys when she was so not into them?

She scooped a pack of Saltine crackers into her lime green Marc Jacobs handbag, straightened her short little green and blue plaid pleated skirt (the best part of the St. Claire's uniform) and left the lunchroom. The route she had to take from lunch to her locker to chemistry was the longest one in the school, up two staircases, around a corner, down another hall . . . blah, blah, blah. She hated to rush, hated to be jabbed and elbowed by the crush of people who were racing to make it to class on time.

Better to leave early. That way she could take her time and engage in her latest favorite hobby as she strolled through the halls: staring at each and every girl at St. Claire's Academy and wondering, *Is she gay?*

Am I *gay?* Heather wondered for the hundredth time that day.

For the past year, she'd been seriously considering that she might be. For one thing, how else to explain the fact that she just didn't seem to be into guys at all? Some guys were okay—as friends—but she had no desire to get up close and personal with any of them. She had dated a few guys her sophomore year, and had made out with one of them. But it was like her battery was dead. She never felt that thing you're supposed to feel.

Girls, on the other hand . . . that was a different story. Lately, she'd been getting a definite buzz when she was around certain female people. Not Marianna or Lisa Marie, of course. That would be way too weird, practically incestuous. They'd been like sisters to her for as long as she'd known them.

But other people . . .

She caught Katie Morgan's eye across the crowded hallway. Was she gay? Heather wondered. Hoped. On days when she admitted the truth, Heather knew she was developing a crush on Katie Morgan, but she had no idea whether it was pointless or not. How was she supposed to find out?

It all started when what she called The Moment happened during a school trip last spring. The St. Claire's Academy Chorale took a trip to New York City to sing with other elite high school choral groups at Lincoln Center. Marianna's father wouldn't let her go—big surprise—and Lisa Marie didn't sing. So Heather wound up rooming with two girls she barely knew.

One of her roommates was Serena Moss, a senior who was openly gay. Serena wasn't exactly beautiful, but she carried herself with such utter assurance that everyone thought of her as gorgeous. Tall, with naturally copper red hair, she was surprisingly busty for a girl with slim bones. Heather, by comparison, was average height, a perfect size eight, with shoulder-length dirty blond hair and no reason to shop for a C cup.

Sharing a room for three days, it was hard not to think about Serena—and hard not to notice her parading around in her underwear. Too often, Heather found herself watching and then wondering: Was it normal to stare? Was Mandy Hartsfield, their other roommate, staring, too? Was it just some sort of hormonal imbalance?

Or did it actually mean something? Was it a memo to Heather, saying: *Wake up. You're gay, too?*

On the second night of the trip, a bunch of girls had gathered in someone's room to drink beers out of the minibar and talk about their plans for the summer. All the seniors were bragging about letting loose, and Serena said, "I'm going to spend a month sunbathing topless on the deck in a tiny villa off the coast of Greece."

"I wish I could go with you," Heather had blurted out.

Whoa. The room had gotten super quiet for a nanosecond, until someone said, "Don't we all," and the awkwardness passed.

Wow, Heather realized. *They all thought I was coming on to her. Was I?* That's what having too much beer could do to her—too much, in Heather's case, being one entire bottle of Heineken. She wasn't much of a boozer or user.

At the end of the evening, right before they went to bed, Mandy pulled out a camera and said, "Group photo!"

Everyone squished together, half the girls sitting on the edge of a bed and the other half kneeling behind them, to get in the picture. Serena draped her arm around Heather and leaned in close. The feeling of skin on skin—Serena's arm across Heather's back and shoulders—sent a charge through her body like she'd never felt before.

"Smile!" Mandy instructed the group.

Not a problem.

Heather grinned like an idiot and hoped Mandy would take two or three more shots, so The Moment would never end. But Mandy got it in one.

"What a great trip, huh?" Serena said as they headed back to their room.

"Yeah." It was all Heather could think to say.

After that, Heather had spent countless weeks trying to figure out what to do with her feelings for girls, hoping they'd just go away. So far, no luck.

It was lonely, though. She couldn't possibly tell Marianna or Lisa Marie that she thought she might be a lesbian. It would change everything.

Or would it?

She was way too scared to find out.

The hallway outside the chemistry lab was crowded with people hanging out before class, dragging their feet about going in because they knew Mr. Norton was a wimp about tardiness.

Heather pushed her way through a clump of girls and was about to go into the room when she saw Katie Morgan on the periphery.

Her throat immediately tightened up. Just being so close to such a beautiful girl made her nervous. Tall, leggy, and gorgeous, with the kind of cascading long blond hair you only see in shampoo commercials, Katie's most stunning feature was her brilliant smile. When she flashed it, you felt like you'd follow her anywhere. Guys were mesmerized by her, and every girl wanted to be her friend.

Could she possibly be gay? Heather wondered again. Probably not. For one thing, she dated guys—Marco Wessington and Eric Sandberg, to name two—although she'd never really gone out with any of them for too long.

Besides, most of the girls in school who were gay were out. If Katie were gay, Heather would know about it. Wouldn't she?

On the other hand, Katie might still be in the closet or, like Heather, not sure how she felt.

Heather had her hopes.

Mr. Norton stuck his head into the hall and made a perfunctory grouchy face, just to get everyone moving. Katie and her friends slowly ambled into the room, and Heather followed, taking a seat at a table in the back.

"Okay, class, we've got a lot of material to cover today," Mr. Norton said. He was wearing a pair of yellow goggles and a starched white lab coat. "I want you to pair up with the person sitting next you, to share a beaker. We're going to be testing for exothermic and endothermic reactions."

Heather glanced to her right and saw Derrick Talbot grinning at her. Oh, please. Not the dumbest guy in the senior class. Heather had already made the mistake of offering to tutor him on a chem project a few months ago—she couldn't help herself, he was so pathetic. Of course, he took it the wrong way and had been flirting with her, calling her, and IM-ing her ever since.

"Cool," Derrick said, looking pleased as punch. "I always thought there was a lot of chemistry between us."

Ugh.

"Well, you were wrong," Katie Morgan said in an I'm-brash-but-I'm-cute sort of way. Katie had been sitting a few seats away, but now she nudged Derrick with her elbow. "Move over. Trade partners with me."

Katie was the kind of beautiful, popular, confident girl you didn't say no to. Derrick gave Heather one last pleading look, hoping she'd bail him out and keep him as her lab partner, but that definitely wasn't happening. Finally, shoulders drooping, he picked up his chem book, which Heather noticed still looked brand-new, as if it had never been opened, and slid onto the next stool.

"Thanks!" Heather whispered, leaning close to Katie so Derrick wouldn't hear.

"Don't thank me," Katie said. "I did it for totally selfish reasons." She beamed at Heather with dancing eyes.

What did that mean? Was she saying she liked Heather? Or just that she wanted to get a good grade on this lab?

Katie's face, eyes, and smile always said, "I love getting what I want." But not in a bad way. Heather found her confidence thrilling.

"So what the hell is an exothermic reaction, anyway?" Katie asked. "I forgot to read this chapter."

"It's something that produces heat," Heather said. Then she blushed because in her head she wanted to add, *Just like you.*

"I'm all for that," Katie said with a bright laugh.

Suddenly, Heather couldn't get enough air. She felt like she'd better hold very still to make sure she didn't do something dumb, or embarrassing, or wrong.

It was weird to feel so excited that she didn't know what to do with herself. Especially in chem class. This was one of her best subjects.

"You'll need safety goggles for this," Mr. Norton was saying. "We're going to start with dilute sulfuric acid . . ."

Katie's arm brushed against Heather's hand as she reached for a pair of goggles.

Did she do that on purpose? Heather glanced over, wondering. Katie's brilliant smile beamed back at her.

The next twenty minutes were a kind of tortured, blissful agony. It physically hurt to be so close to Katie, but still, Heather didn't want class to end. She couldn't concentrate, though, and accidentally poured too much magnesium powder into their beaker. Katie didn't seem to care.

"It looks like the gunk that comes out of that creature's jaw in *Alien,*" Katie said about the green chemicals bubbling up. "Hey, do you want to come over and watch that movie with me on Friday?"

Heather froze. Was Katie asking her for a date? If so, she desperately wanted to say yes. It would be such a relief to finally be true to herself. But what if it wasn't a date? Heather couldn't bear the thought of making a fool of herself.

She could see it all now: she'd get to Katie's and not know where to sit. On the couch or the floor? Close to Katie or halfway across the room? She wouldn't know what to wear, how to talk, whether to flirt when Katie offered her a bowl of popcorn, or just eat it and shut up.

"Um, I can't," Heather said. "I've got other stuff I have to do."

"Okay." Katie shrugged, only slightly disappointed.

Heather wanted to disappear.

Other stuff? Had she actually said "other stuff"? Next thing, she'd be grunting and using sign language. Heather hated herself for acting like such a social loser.

Funny, I'm never uncomfortable like this with guys, Heather thought.

Maybe that meant something, she decided. Maybe she was better with guys. Maybe she wasn't really a lesbian at all.

Chapter 4

"Hey, girl. Looks like you pulled it together," Graham said when Lisa Marie showed up for her second day as a Starbucks partner.

"Huh?" Lisa Marie pretended she didn't know what he was talking about. Just because her face had been all red and puffy when she came in to work last Saturday didn't mean she wasn't totally ready to handle a stupid little job like making coffee. After all, she'd set a record learning how to make all sixty-eight kinds of Starbucks beverages, hadn't she?

"You were a mess last time," Graham said with a shrug. "Gary wasn't sure he was going to keep you, even though you did learn all the pumps in one day."

Wow. Lisa Marie hadn't realized that a tiny little bit of crying on the job was grounds for dismissal. She had only sniffled once. Or twice.

Anyway, she was in a much better mood now. Ever since this morning, when word spread through school that she was single again, guys had been paying a lot more attention to her. She was almost positive that one of the hottest guys at St. Claire's, Marco Wessington, had smiled at her on his way to his locker. Marco Wessington! His father was a congressman. Marco knew he was all that, so Lisa Marie had always thought he was out of her league. But maybe not.

She stood behind the counter refilling the skim milk containers and wiping down espresso drips from the prep surface, ready to call out the coffee orders. Too bad the counter was so high. It hid her best feature, her navel, which showed pretty nicely in the low-cut black pants she was wearing. Well, maybe she could get out from behind the counter to wipe down some tables or refill the cinnamon shaker or something.

"You need an apron," Graham reminded, handing her one. "They're required. And your shirt has to be long enough to tuck in. Make sure, next time."

So much for her best feature.

A jazz mix CD was playing on the sound system. Lisa Marie moved in time to the Latin beat, wishing someone would come in and order something. It was so boring doing all the grunt work Graham gave her when the place was empty. Restocking the retail shelves, cleaning out the prep sinks, hauling huge containers of milk from the stockroom fridge to the bar—it was all dreary.

Dealing with customers was so much more fun.

As if her prayers were being answered, the door opened, and two guys from St. Claire's Academy walked in: John somebody and Ramone. They were inseparable, the school's two most cliché jocks. John was on the lacrosse, basketball, soccer, and swim teams. He wore a numbered jersey of some sort every day of the year. Ramone played basketball like he owned the court.

"Hey," John said, grinning at her as he approached the counter. "What's good here?"

"I'd try the tomato juice," Lisa Marie joked.

"I'll take it if you'll squeeze it yourself," John said, clearly flirting with her.

"Squeeze it?" Ramone sounded seriously confused. "You don't squeeze tomato juice, do you?"

Lisa Marie and John burst out laughing.

"*Somebody's* got to squeeze it," John shot back. "But, uh, give me a tall double espresso. I'll make it easy today."

"Make that two," Ramone chimed in, as if he'd never had a single original thought in his life.

"Two tall double espressos," Lisa Marie called out to Graham.

John and Ramone paid, then slouched toward the end of the counter to wait for their drinks. When Lisa Marie bent over to get the next customer a muffin, she could feel the guys watching her through the glass case. She could also feel her apron strings dangling across her bare skin, where her cute little Juicy Couture shirt was riding up in back.

"Nice apron," Ramone called out with a grin.

How come Todd never said anything like that, never made her feel like she looked sexy?

Lisa Marie was liking this job more and more every second.

The next two customers were older women, her mother's age, and they barely made eye contact. But a few minutes later, Bradley Boulter came in carrying his tennis racket. Bradley was too short, too sweet, and too wimpy to be labeled a jock like John and Ramone, but he was an awesome tennis player who took the team to the regionals. He was always ditching school to fly across the country for elite-level tournaments.

"Hi," Bradley said, "when did you start working here?"

"This is my second day." It came out sounding like she was proud to have held down a job that long. Well, she was.

"Can I get one of those iced tea drinks?" Bradley asked.

"Which one?"

"The fruity pink one."

Lisa Marie placed the drink order properly and waited while he fished money out of his pocket.

"So how'd they get you to work here, anyway?" Bradley asked. "I mean, did the sign in the window say, 'Hot Chick Wanted'?"

Lisa Marie blushed. This was amazing! Guys were actually hitting on her now that she and Todd were broken up. Who knew being single could be so much fun?

For the next two hours, she worked the counter and "worked it" with all the private school boys who came in to have coffee. St. Claire's wasn't the only feeder school for this particular Starbucks. There were guys from Sidwell Friends and The Field School, too.

Graham offered her a break at 6:45, after what he called "frappy hour," but she wasn't in the mood for a break. Not with all these cool guys hanging around.

"No thanks . . . I mean, no *thank you,*" Lisa Marie corrected herself quickly. "I'm not tired."

"Okay. You cover. I'm going outside for a smoke," Graham said.

A few minutes later the door swung open, and Marianna and Heather came in, looking all proud of themselves for showing up, as if she'd never in a million years have expected to see them there.

"We came to keep you company," Heather announced brightly.

"Yeah, hang out, moral support," Marianna added.

It was a nice gesture but totally unnecessary. Lisa Marie wasn't even sure she wanted them hanging around while she tried out her new skill—namely, flirting with all the hot guys. Who needed an audience for that?

And besides, the place was buzzing.

"You two are the best," she said. "But honestly, I'm kinda too busy to talk right now."

It was true: Graham was outside, so she was temporarily on her own behind the bar. She was hustling like crazy to get all the drinks made.

"That's okay, we'll just hang out," Marianna said. "I'll have a tall skim milk cappuccino."

"Is that to go or stay?"

Marianna looked hurt. "To stay. What did you think I meant by 'hang out'?"

Oh, boy.

"She's just nervous, it's only her second day." Heather said.

Thanks, Lisa Marie thought. Heather could always be counted on to make nice. She was awesome at smoothing over the rough spots in relationships. Even when Lisa Marie was feeling especially premenstrual, rattling on and on about Todd, or the prom, or obsessing about getting the perfect dress, Heather never made her feel like she was being an attention hog.

"So what do I want?" Heather said, gazing up at the menu board. She stared and stared, with a distant look on her face, like she was thinking about something else.

"Yes?" Lisa Marie waited.

"Huh?"

"You were ordering."

"Oh. Yeah. Sorry," Heather snapped back to the present. "Um . . . I don't know. Surprise me, okay?"

"Well, it's kind of hard to surprise you," Lisa Marie pointed out with a laugh. "I have to call out the drink order and then, normally, about four other people would call it out, too, while they rang it up and made it. But since I'm here alone right now, I'll see what I can do."

"Thanks." Heather put a five dollar bill on the counter and said, "Keep the change."

"Ew, no. That's creepy, taking tips from my best friends."

"Just this once," Heather promised. "From now on, you give us extra shots in all our coffees."

Lisa Marie made Marianna's cappuccino and tried to think of what to give Heather, but she kept getting distracted. A crowd of guys from Sidwell Friends had been hanging out at a corner table for more than an hour, and they kept watching her, like they wanted to talk or something. How was she supposed to give them her full attention with her girlfriends around?

And then the door opened, and in walked the one guy she'd had a crush on since forever. Drew Hammond, St. Claire's Academy's only honest-to-god hip-hop talent—a guy who even the teachers acknowledged was likely to make it big—was there with two guys from his posse. Otherwise known as Li'l D, Drew had been performing in small clubs around D.C. for more than a year, and the rumor was that an indie label wanted to sign him.

With his smooth, bony cheekbones, gaunt face, wild dreadlocks, and latte-colored skin, he was the hottest thing Lisa Marie had ever seen.

Her mind spun as she tried to think of something to say that would sound cool. What do you say to someone who's practically already a celebrity?

Without thinking, she just poured a regular coffee for Heather, set it on the bar without even calling it, and went to take Li'l D's order.

"Hi," she said, wondering whether to call him Li'l D or Drew.

The thing about Drew was that there was nothing little about him. His nickname was a total goof. The story went that three of the guys in his posse all had names starting with D: Dave, Damien, and Durran. They were all shorter than he was, so they gave him the name Li'l D as a joke, and it stuck.

"Hi." Li'l D's eyes were deep. He really looked at you, Lisa Marie thought, like he was seeing into your heart and soul, or reading your mind or something.

Lisa Marie flashed him her best smile and turned on the charm. Who cared if her friends were watching, and his buddies were standing right behind him? This was her chance to flirt with him.

"What can I get you?" She made it sound like it meant more than it did.

A smile flickered on Li'l D's luscious mouth. "How about a skim milk cappuccino with a double shot of espresso?" he said. He glanced up at the menu, then met her eyes again. "What size should I get?"

"You obviously need a big one," Lisa Marie answered quickly.

What did that even mean? She couldn't believe she was being so bold and out there. It was almost embarrassing.

But it seemed to be working. Li'l D grinned at her, and his buddies were smirking.

She held his gaze, not wanting the moment to end.

"Okay. Give me a big one, then," he said.

Out of the corner of her eye, she saw someone approach the counter and pick up the coffee she'd set there.

"Is this for me?" Heather called.

Lisa Marie half nodded without looking over.

"Well, okay, then," Heather said, clearing her throat. She motioned to Marianna, pointing toward the door. "I guess we'll see you later."

"Bye," Lisa Marie called, barely nodding as they left.

To be honest, she was glad to see them go.

The thing about girlfriends, Lisa Marie thought, was that they were always there for you—even when you didn't want them to be.

Chapter 5

"I'm eighteen, Dad," Marianna pleaded, hating the sound of her own whiny voice. "I'm going away to college in six months! It's insane not to let me go out to a movie with a boy. You can't keep me locked up here forever!"

"You may or may not be going *away* to college." Her father raised a threatening eyebrow.

Oh, wow. Was he stooping to that threat already?

"You're saying I can't go to Wash U?" Marianna's mouth dropped open.

"We still haven't settled that, you know," her father said.

It was a low blow, and everyone in the living room felt it. Marianna's mother, who always sat silently through these arguments and couldn't be counted on to swat down a fly let alone argue with her husband, stiffened visibly. Even her thirteen-year-old brother Max was quieter than usual.

Everyone knew she'd already been accepted at Washington University in Saint Louis, her first-choice school. This was just a tactic—one of her father's favorites. He was determined to keep her obedient and under his thumb as long as possible, so whenever she acted the least bit independent, he floated the idea that maybe she should go to Georgetown instead, and live at home.

It was horrible and mean-spirited, and she didn't really think he'd go through with it. But how could she know for sure?

Why am I taking the bait? she thought. She was letting him get her off topic. She didn't have time to be distracted. Her date with Luke was tomorrow night—she'd already waited too long to face her father and get his permission. She needed to stay focused on the subject at hand.

"It's just a movie," Marianna repeated. She was trying to stay calm—she really was—but she could feel the panic rising in her throat. It was already 8:30 on Thursday night. How was she going to tell Luke that the date was off, the night before they were supposed to go out? "I'm graduating in two months! Come on, Dad."

"I don't see any reason to bend the rules now," her father said, swirling his glass of leftover Merlot.

"Er . . ." Marianna's mother cleared her throat softly, trying to speak up. All heads turned. She had never contradicted her husband before.

"Yes?" Her father's eyes dared her mother to keep speaking.

"Um, it probably wouldn't hurt to let her go out to one movie, Harold," she said meekly. "You want her to get some experience with boys while you're still here to guide her, don't you?"

Wow. Marianna couldn't remember her mother ever standing up for her before.

Harold shot his wife a fleeting look that was hard to read. Marianna wondered if they'd have a fight later. Her dad could get really furious sometimes. He'd never admit it, but he needed anger management lessons. He was a first-class bully.

"All right. If that's what you think, Adrianna. I'll take your advice. Let's hope it doesn't turn out to be an enormous mistake."

You could cut the tension in the room with a knife.

"Thanks, Daddy!" Marianna leapt up to give him a hug. She hadn't called him Daddy in more than three years. She turned to run upstairs, to call her friends and tell them the amazing news. She was going on a date with Luke. A real date!

"But you'll have to be home by 9:30," he said sternly, stopping her in her tracks.

Was he kidding? Was he completely insane?

"No way." She whirled around angrily, her voice thin and high. "That's ridiculous, and you know it. How can you treat me like a total child?"

Uh-oh. Her father's scowl was enough to make her sorry she'd said a word.

"If you can't control your temper, Marianna, maybe you're not old enough to have dating privileges at all," he warned.

"It's not even a date if I have to be home that early!" Marianna complained. "It's more like he's babysitting me!"

"Who is this boy, anyway?" Her father raised his voice, and raised the stakes at the same time. The message was clear: He could change his mind at any minute if he didn't like the sound of this guy.

"He's on the cross-country team." She knew the minute she said it that she was in dangerous territory.

"That's what I thought." Her father looked smug. "I've always said that boys who play sports with girls are only after one thing."

Here we go. Marianna wanted to die. She couldn't bear another one of his lectures about guys—not now. Not with her little brother smirking from his perch on a chair arm. What was he doing hanging around for this conversation anyway? It was none of his business.

"Don't you have something better to do?" she snapped at Max.

"Yeah. Can I go over to Neil's house to watch *The Matrix*?" he asked his dad.

"Yes." Her father nodded without an instant's debate.

"I don't believe this!" Marianna screeched, pointing at

the antique clock on the mantel. "It's almost nine o'clock—on a school night! How come he's allowed to stay out later than me?"

Her father glared, angry that she was even demanding an explanation from him. "Max is not going to be assaulted walking three blocks to a friend's house," he said in a cold, patronizing tone. "I'm sorry, Marianna, but I didn't set up the way the world works. Girls are more vulnerable; that's a simple fact. Now do you want to go on this date tomorrow night, or do you want to argue with me? It's a choice. One or the other."

A choice? That was a laugh. What choice did she ever have?

She stormed out of the living room, stomped up the steps to her room, and slammed the door. Big protest. Even she was embarrassed by how lame it was.

But at least she was going to be allowed to go out with Luke. She just hoped he would understand about the curfew.

She opened her e-mail and found a note from him in her in-box.

> Hi—How about I pick you up at 7:30 tomorrow night? The film starts at 8:10. Maybe we can get a pizza after, unless you're one of those girls who doesn't eat. (In which case, I'm going to totally whip your ass at the cross-country trials next week, you'll be so weak from hunger.) ☻—Luke

Marianna's head throbbed. *The film starts at 8:10.* How was she supposed to be home by 9:30? There was no possible way.

Trembling, she hit the Reply button and started to answer Luke's e-mail, but a moment later he showed up on her Buddy List. Maybe IM-ing him was easier.

MKazanjian: Hey Luke

LPerchik: hi, you. r u running tomorrow a.m.?

MKazanjian: yeah.

LPerchik: better watch out. I'll be flying. Is 7:30 okay to pick you up tomorrow nite?

MKazanjian: sure, but there's a problem. I have to be home by 9:30. Can you believe that?

MKazanjian: Luke? You still there?

MKazanjian: hello?

LPerchik: sorry . . . gotta take a call from my dad. back in a sec . . .

Marianna waited more like a thousand seconds, but he didn't come back to the chat. Obviously, he had dumped her. She couldn't honestly blame him. What guy wanted to go out with a girl who had a *bedtime*?

Then an e-mail from Luke popped up in her in-box.

Hi—Sorry, the movie doesn't get out till 9:45. Maybe you'd be better off with a matinee instead—Luke

A matinee? A movie in the afternoon, when only little kids were there? How completely and utterly humiliating. He was mocking her, of course, probably to make himself feel better about canceling their date. No doubt he'd spread the news all over school first thing the next morning. Tell everyone that she wasn't allowed to stay out past frigging 9:30 on a Friday night. She might as well crawl into a hole and die.

Her cell phone rang in her purse, and she dove for it. Maybe he was calling to apologize?

Nope. It was only Heather.

"Hi," Marianna said, too embarrassed to tell her what had happened with Luke. "What's up?"

"I'm at Lisa Marie's, and we're studying for the American lit midterm. Can we borrow your notes on *Moby-Dick*?"

"Sure," Marianna said, agreeing to e-mail the notes. She changed the subject. "But you've got to promise me something. Promise me we'll all go to the prom as a group, like we planned."

"Definitely," Heather said. "I'm pumped for that."

Not that Marianna's dad was going to let her stay out late on prom night. She'd have to really work on him to even let her go with a group of girls at all. But at least she'd be there, and she'd have on a killer dress, and she'd make Luke sorry he'd treated her like a kid.

In the background, Marianna heard Heather repeating the message to Lisa Marie, who agreed weakly.

"Thank you," Marianna said. "You two are the best. You always say the right things."

But just in case they didn't, she would wait until tomorrow to tell them how Luke had dumped her.

Chapter 6

"Squeeze in, everyone," Mr. Rayburn told the third period civics class the next morning as he wrote a list of terms on the chalkboard and waved people into the room. "Mr. Young was called away for an emergency, so we're combining both groups today."

Chairs squeaked and tables groaned across the linoleum floor.

"Mr. Young's people, just push those tables against the wall—you can sit on them," Mr. Rayburn said.

Marianna glanced up from the civics chapter she had been skimming, trying to cram during the five minutes before class started—which was what happened when she was so pissed at someone, she blew off the reading the night before. She spotted Luke, the very someone she was pissed at, standing in the doorway to the classroom.

He met her eyes with a question, but she looked away quickly. Was he wondering why she had skipped tempo training that morning? Easy one. Tempo training was optional on Fridays. Why show up and give him another chance to humiliate her?

The room echoed with desks and tables being pushed back and scooted around. When the crowd settled, Luke was sitting knees up, back against the wall, on the floor, directly in her line of sight.

She kept her head bent, skimming the chapter over and over but not taking in a word of it.

"So who can tell me what the Supreme Court's role was in deciding the 2000 election?" Mr. Rayburn asked. "And how does it demonstrate our system of checks and balances?"

Marianna's hand went up. "It doesn't. The Supreme Court took control of the voting process and determined the outcome of the election," she said. "If it hadn't been for—"

"No, I'm not asking a political question," Mr. Rayburn interrupted her. "I'm talking about how each branch of the government has separate powers and responsibilities."

Great. Now Rayburn was dismissing her like a child, in front of Luke.

Luke's hand shot up while Mr. Rayburn was still talking.

"Yes?" Rayburn called on him.

"Marianna's right," Luke said. "The system is supposed to have checks and balances, but they didn't work in the 2000 election because the court decided the whole thing. The court shouldn't be deciding our elections . . ."

His voice trailed off, and someone else chimed in on the debate, but Marianna wasn't really listening. Her heart was pumping a little irregular rhythm, and she was holding her own internal debate on a much more important issue: Should she look over at Luke right now and smile?

He had defended her! That had to mean something good, didn't it?

Maybe he hadn't been mocking her last night with that matinee comment after all. Maybe he really meant it. Could he possibly want to go to an afternoon movie?

She doodled pictures of King Kong, the movie they were supposed to go see, through the rest of the class. Finally the bell rang.

Luke was first out the door, but he was waiting for her in the hallway.

"Hi," he said. "I missed you this morning."

"Yeah, well, I thought I'd take a break," she said cautiously. She wanted to say, *I missed you, too,* but she wasn't in the mood to go out on any limbs. "That was nice in class—you backing me up."

"You were right," Luke said. "These teachers who don't want to get into political discussions drive me crazy. What's the point of learning civics?"

He jerked his head toward the main hallway. "I have Spanish. You going that way?"

Marianna shook her head. Her next class was in the opposite direction.

Luke shrugged. "Okay, well . . ."

Was he just going to walk off without saying a thing about their date? Was it on or off?

"So do you want to maybe study for the civics exam after school today?" he said. "We could do it before nine thirty p.m. Daylight saving time doesn't even start until next weekend."

Unbelievable. He was mocking her again!

Marianna spun around and started to stomp away, but Luke grabbed her arm.

"Hey, wait, wait. I was just kidding. What's wrong?"

"You're trying to make me feel like a jerk about my curfew," Marianna snapped. "That crack about going to a matinee? If you want to get out of our date, just say so."

His blue eyes opened wide. "No. No, I don't want to get out of our date," he said quickly. "I was serious about the matinee. If that works better for you, then let's just go tomorrow afternoon."

"Seriously?"

He nodded, and since he was still holding on to the arm of her sweater, he gave it a little tug. "Meet me after school by the statue, and we'll figure it out."

Then he flashed his irresistible smile at her one more time and hurried down the hall.

Marianna felt happier inside than she could remember feeling in a long time. Suddenly, everything about St. Claire's Academy seemed . . . what was the word? *Nice*. The hallways, with their wooden wainscot paneling and old stone floors were nice. The heavy doorways leading from the west corridor and down a flight of steps were nice. Having a calculus quiz right before lunch was nice because . . . she had to think hard to come up with a reason . . . because it meant she didn't have to worry about taking it in the afternoon. The smell of macaroni and cheese bubbling in the cafeteria kitchen? Nice. It reminded her of grade school.

Floating, she found her way to her next class without even thinking about how she got there. All she could think about was Luke. His cute smile; his hard, muscular chest; the way he bent his head slightly when he was talking to her. What a relief to finally talk *up* to a guy.

The only problem was her dad, but she had decided there was no way she'd let that be an issue. She simply wouldn't tell him about her dates. Nope. She was going to see Luke on the sly, and let her father think she was just spending lots of time with Lisa Marie and Heather.

She had it all figured out—except for one thing.

What if Luke asked her to the prom? She'd already made Heather and Lisa Marie *swear* they'd go as a group.

No, if things worked out with Luke, she was going to have to come up with a new plan. Maybe she, Lisa Marie, and Heather could go to prom as a group . . . but then meet up with various guys when they got there. That could work. From the looks of things at Starbucks, Lisa Marie was going to have to fight guys off with a stick.

Heather was another story, though. She didn't really seem to be trying.

Marianna and Lisa Marie would have to put their heads together and come up with someone for Heather; that's all there was to it.

Instant message:

MKazanjian: hey, Heather girl. guess who gave me a back rub while we were studying after school today?

HProule: Who?!!!

MKazanjian: Luke. He is so amazing.

HProule: Unbelievable! Where were you?????

MKazanjian: On the steps of the Lincoln Memorial. Luke said it would inspire us to ace our civics test.

HProule: Did it?

MKazanjian: no, we didn't even study. but it inspired me to lie to my dad three times in one phone conversation.

HProule: LOL

LMSantos: hey, Marianna.

MKazanjian: hey, coffee queen! Why r'nt you at Starbucks?

LMSantos: Graham took me off the schedule this weekend. He's punishing me.

HProule: what for?

LMSantos: forgetting to call somebody's drink.

MKazanjian: bad girl.

LMSantos: right. phone the coffee police. anyway, why aren't you on your date with Luke?

MKazanjian: we're going out tomorrow, so my dad won't have a cow about it. BTW, if he calls, I'm studying with both of you tomorrow.

LMSantos: that's cool

MKazanjian: Listen, I was thinking about the prom. When we get there, I might want to hang with Luke part of the time, you know?

LMSantos: totally. We shouldn't be tied down to each other.

MKazanjian: don't worry, Heather, we'll find someone for you.

LMSantos: def. we won't abandon you, girl.

MKazanjian: someone better than Derrick what'sisface

LMSantos: someone you'll really like

MKazanjian: so you'll have an awesome time . . .

LMSantos: what about Eric Lorber?

MKazanjian: oooh. good idea.

LMSantos: we'll think of something

MKazanjian: any ideas, Heather girl?

LMSantos: Heather? you there?

MKazanjian: Hello??????

Chapter 7

Katie Morgan had the most perfectly shaped head on the planet, and Heather couldn't stop staring at it. Katie was four rows in front of her in French class. Her head rose like a jewel on the long stem of her neck, and sat there on display, like an exhibit in a museum. Even from the back, with her silky blond hair cascading over her shoulders, the shape of her head was simply spectacular.

I bet she'll look amazing in her prom dress, Heather thought, imagining something strapless.

Heather had already bought her own dress for the prom, the green beaded flapper thing she'd tried on a few weeks ago when Lisa Marie was obsessing in BCBG. It wasn't the typical look other St. Claire's girls would be wearing, which was why Heather loved it. Who wanted to be one of the

Stepford girls, sucking up to other people's trends? Better to be original. Not so everyone else would follow you, but so they wouldn't.

If only she could make Katie follow her somewhere . . . anywhere . . .

For the past five days, Heather had been desperately trying to read the signs, trying to figure out whether she and Katie were ever going to happen. But it was like reading tea leaves. There were signals, but what did they really mean?

Sure, Katie was really friendly to her lately. Ever since they'd been paired up as lab partners, she'd been smiling every time she passed Heather in the halls, making small talk in the cafeteria line, asking to borrow Heather's eyeliner in the restroom.

But was Katie flirting with her? Or just being nice? Did it *mean* something when Katie passed by at lunch and fixed the label in Heather's shirt—something other than *Your label is out, you stupid geek*?

And what about all those guys Katie was nice to? Randall Devalier got at least as much face time with Katie as Heather did.

Now there was an awful thought. What if Katie went to the prom with a guy?

There was only one thing she knew for sure: Now that Katie was on her radar screen, Heather didn't want to lie to herself about being gay. Not that she was ready to let anyone else know. That would be way too scary. But at least she wasn't going to deny her own feelings inside the privacy of her own head.

The bell finally rang for the end of class. Heather leapt up, hoping to bump into Katie on the way out, but it didn't happen. Katie was gone pretty fast.

Marianna caught up with Heather in the hallway. "I saw who you were watching during class," she announced with a knowing grin.

Heather froze. Her throat felt tight. This was the moment she'd been trying to avoid. But Marianna was grinning, totally pleased with herself.

"Who?"

"Tony." Marianna beamed. "And I can see why. He's perfect for you!"

Tony? It took a second for Heather to even process the name. Tony Vilanch? Why on earth . . . ?

Oh, right. He was sitting two seats over from Katie.

"Hmm," Heather said, trying to bluff a mild interest even though all she could think was, *Don't get carried away, Marianna.*

She headed toward her locker on the way to lunch. Marianna followed.

"Don't you think he's perfect for you?" Marianna sounded hurt that her brainstorm wasn't being met with jubilation. "I mean, seriously. He's the ultimate metrosexual. You and he have so much in common."

"Like what?"

"Oh, you know. Everything," Marianna said. "He's on the staff of the lit mag, isn't he?"

"So what?"

Heather stuffed her books in her locker and slammed it.

"I think he does illustrations," Marianna said. "And you do layout for the yearbook. You're both arty."

"Yeah, but . . ."

"No buts. He's perfect! He's just like you: great looking, sensitive . . ."

Marianna was on a roll, and there was no stopping her.

"He hangs with the hipster crowd," Heather said, not really complaining, but trying to prove that he wasn't *just* like her.

"Mostly the filmmaking crowd," Marianna corrected her. "But he's not so touch-me-not as the hard-core hipsters are. Also, big point: he's available."

They had reached the cafeteria, and Lisa Marie overheard the last part of the conversation. Naturally she jumped right in. "Who's available?"

Marianna rolled her eyes. "Don't get greedy, I'm fixing Heather up for the prom."

"For the prom! Who said anything about the prom?" Heather gasped. She turned, pleading, to Lisa Marie. "She's trying to hook me up with Tony Vilanch." It was said in a save-me tone of voice calculated to make Lisa Marie take her side, but it didn't work. Lisa Marie caught some kind of coded glance from Marianna.

I know what they're up to, Heather thought. It was obvious they thought they were being nice, doing her a favor. But she really didn't want this kind of help.

"Tony? He's definitely available," Lisa Marie said.

"Oh, right. If you call moping around for a year available," Heather said. "He's been quote unquote 'available' ever since Jenny Burkowski broke his heart last year."

Heather didn't need to elaborate. Everyone knew the story. Tony and Jenny had been a couple for a full eight months until she dumped him the week before the prom. (Apparently someone forgot to tell *her* about Rule #1.) Clearly, he was still desperate to get back with her, since he hadn't hooked up with anyone else.

So now they wanted Heather to go after him, huh? She didn't know whether to be flattered or annoyed. What made her friends think she could score with Tony, anyway? To say nothing—absolutely nothing—about the fact that she didn't want to.

"I asked around," Marianna said, reading Heather's mind. "He's going to the prom with a group of guys. So, like I said, he's available."

What could she say? They had her cornered.

"Unless you have someone else in mind?" Lisa Marie asked.

Well, as a matter of fact, she did. But she wasn't about to cough up the truth.

"No," she said.

No one to speak of, anyway.

Chapter 8

"Drive slow. I'm still pulling up my tights, and they're giving me a wedgie," Marianna said, scooting down low in the front seat of Heather's Saturn.

"Well, hurry up. There's Luke," Heather said, pulling into the parking lot at the Retro Metro where Marianna was meeting Luke for their matinee date.

Marianna peered out the front window and saw him leaning against his car, a bright blue ten-year-old Volvo sedan. You could always tell what kind of parents someone had from the cars they bought their kids, Marianna thought.

Marianna, of course, had no car. Case closed.

"Can't you circle or something?" she begged, trying desperately to adjust her panties without being seen.

"He's already spotted us," Heather said. "Just hurry."

Quickly Marianna made the necessary adjustments and checked the visor mirror one more time. When Heather had picked her up half an hour ago—using the cover story that they were studying together that afternoon—Marianna had been wearing old jeans and a Washington U T-shirt. But now she had changed in the car into a cute, flirty skirt and a chocolaty brown cropped top that matched her eyes. Her hair was flowing all over the place, but she had to admit it looked pretty good that way.

"Thanks for driving me," Marianna said before hopping out of the car. "You are the best."

"Have fun," Heather called. "Call me if you want a ride home."

Luke was standing across the parking lot, leaning against the car, arms crossed on his chest. He didn't move to come meet her. He just smiled at her the whole time she walked toward him.

"You look amazing," he said when she was close enough to see the warmth in his eyes. "I love watching you walk. I never get to see you from this side."

Marianna shook her head slightly. She didn't get it. "Hmm?"

"You're always running, either beside me or ahead of me," Luke said. "I spend a lot of time eating your dust, you know."

She laughed. "Well, pick up your feet, Perchik!" She imitated Coach Robinson's voice.

"Not that I mind the rear view," Luke added with a smile.

He took her hand and led her toward the movie theater. He'd already bought the tickets so they wouldn't have to wait on line. Marianna wanted to act cool, but she couldn't stop grinning. He was being so sweet. She was already having more fun than she'd ever had in her life—and the date had barely started!

"Are you a butter girl or a plain girl?" Luke asked, steering her toward the concession stand.

"Right now, I'm a Raisinets girl," Marianna said. "I need dessert. I just had lunch."

"Good idea." Luke bought them a box of Raisinets and two bottles of water, and then they found seats in the back of the theater.

Marianna's heart started beating faster. She'd read in *Cosmo Girl!* that couples who were planning a heavy make-out session always sat in the last row of movie seats, so that no one would be watching from behind.

She was hoping Luke would kiss her, but was she ready for a lot more?

Her pulse quickened at the thought. Yeah, she was!

Luckily, the place wasn't too crowded, and there were zero little kids in the audience, so Marianna didn't feel out of place.

Luke let her go into the row first, acting the gentleman. She took a seat kind of near the wall. He sat close, leaned his shoulder against hers, and opened the Raisinets.

Marianna took just one. She didn't feel like eating anything right now, with Luke so close. How was he going to kiss her if she was feeding her face?

But he didn't kiss her. Not right then. The previews came on, and he just confidently wrapped his arm around her shoulder to hold her close. Marianna loved it, sitting there in his arms, wondering what was going to happen next. It was so much sexier this way.

Then they got caught up in the movie, and she forgot all about kissing him until the scene where King Kong was looking lovingly at Jessica Lange like he wanted her to understand his inner soul or something. Suddenly, she remembered where she was, remembered whose arm was around her shoulder. At the same exact moment, Luke took his free hand, turned Marianna's face toward him gently, and kissed her. The movie faded away. Marianna never wanted the kiss to end, and it almost didn't.

When the movie music made a dramatic crescendo, they both looked at the screen to see what was happening, and went back to watching King Kong raging through the jungle, doing his best impersonation of Marianna's father. Hah! At least, it made her feel rebellious (in a good way) to think of it like that.

Before she knew it, the movie was over.

"You want to take a walk in the park across the street?" Luke asked.

She nodded. The sky was clear, and the air was cool. Marianna couldn't believe how easy it was to talk to him. For one thing, they had a million things in common. He loved old movies and indoor swimming pools, just like she did. (It made them both think of their childhoods, when they went to so many birthday sleepover parties in hotels, and swam in disgustingly steamy, overchlorinated, indoor pools.) He hated two things that were her biggest pet peeves: mushy French toast and people who littered.

They both stopped to pick up small bits of trash that were littering the park.

And of course they both loved cross-country. She could talk to him about running all day, and not get tired of it.

"So where are you going next year?" Luke asked her.

"Wash U." *Assuming my father doesn't decide to completely ruin my life*, she thought. "You?"

"I'll probably be here at Georgetown. They have a great poli-sci program," he explained. "It wasn't my first choice. I was jonesing to go to MIT, but I didn't get in."

Marianna couldn't stop smiling at this guy. Who else would just flat-out admit that they didn't get in to their first-choice school? Most people at St. Claire's were so worried about looking like losers, they wouldn't even reveal which schools they'd applied to until after the April acceptance letters arrived.

Luke was just so . . . there was no other word for him. Special.

He bent down to pick a wildflower, then tucked it behind

her ear. "This is for someone who's usually moving too fast to stop and smell the roses," he said.

"I should slow down sometimes," Marianna said, not even sure what that meant. But it sounded good.

"How about next weekend?" Luke said. "You want to go out again?"

"It'll have to be in the afternoon," she said.

"*Love in the Afternoon*," Luke said. "That's my mom's favorite movie. She cries every time. You ever seen it?"

Marianna shook her head.

"We should rent it sometime," Luke said. "But not next Saturday. I'm more up for whipping your ass at Ping-Pong. You want to come over and see if you can take me?"

"You're on, Perchik," Marianna said eagerly. "But let me warn you: I am killer at Ping-Pong. Be prepared to die."

Luke laughed, covering his eyes and shaking his head. "Oh, no. Don't tell me you can whip me at *two* sports."

Marianna giggled to herself. The truth was, she was terrible at Ping-Pong. She could barely return the ball. But it was just too much fun, teasing Luke and making him think otherwise for a whole week.

"We'll see," she said, her eyes dancing. "We'll just see."

It took Heather twenty minutes to get to the theater to pick Marianna up, so by the time they were driving home it was almost dinnertime. Marianna was worried. She didn't want her dad grilling her about why she was gone so long.

On the other hand, she never wanted to get out of the car, because then she'd have to stop talking about Luke.

"He's so amazing!" she gushed to Heather. "I can't believe I got this lucky."

"That's cool," Heather said.

Marianna just sat there, grinning. She'd been smiling so much, her face almost hurt. "It was so romantic when he kissed me," she told Heather. "It was at the perfect moment. I couldn't help wondering if he'd planned it, you know? Right when King Kong was feeling all romantic about Jessica Lange. He's a great kisser, too."

"Who is—King Kong?"

"Ha-ha. But seriously, I've never kissed anyone who had such great lips."

"You haven't kissed anyone since eighth grade!" Heather reminded her.

"Don't be so literal," Marianna complained.

Okay, it was true. She hadn't kissed that many guys. Okay, only two. And both of them were in junior high. But so what? This was magical, and she intended to enjoy it. What was up with Heather, anyway? It was like she didn't seem to get, or really care, how wonderful Luke was.

Heather was obviously bored with the topic, too, because she changed the subject.

"So do you want to hear the rumor that's going around about why Todd broke up with Lisa Marie?" Heather said.

"What?" Marianna's eyes opened wide. Heather didn't usually gossip, so this must be big.

"I heard from a reliable source that he dumped her so he could ask Delia Apfelbaum to the prom."

"You're kidding!" Delia was a bit of a reach for Todd. "Who told you?" The question came out, out of habit, but Marianna knew it was pointless. Heather was very discreet. Like the perfect Washington diplomat, she never revealed her sources.

"It's just what I heard," Heather said.

"I wonder if Lisa Marie knows," Marianna asked.

"I'm not sure, but anyway, it doesn't matter. The word is that Delia turned him down."

"Duh."

Well, this was an interesting development, Marianna thought, wondering how Lisa Marie was going to feel about the news.

Lisa Marie wasn't exactly the type to gloat over her ex's failures.

But then again, she wasn't exactly the type *not* to gloat, either.

Chapter 9

"Isn't that the fourth guy you just agreed to meet at the prom?" Graham asked Lisa Marie as she wiped the counters at Starbucks on Saturday.

The store had finally gotten quiet after a big rush, and Lisa Marie was practically glowing. Guys from her school had been coming in all day, flirting like crazy, competing for her attention. Hard as it was to believe, Lisa Marie seemed to be the center of the Starbucks universe—and she was loving it.

Starbucks was raining men!

But that didn't mean she was going to start acting like a slut.

Was Graham right? Had she actually agreed to meet four different guys at the prom?

"Noooo," she said, shaking her head slowly. "I don't think so. Wait. Who?"

"Last week, that guy with the tennis racket," Graham said, ticking them off on his fingers. "He was the first."

"Bradley?" Lisa Marie had already forgotten about him. Yeah, when she thought back, she had to admit that she *had* said yes when he asked her to hang with him at the prom. "Oh, but he was just . . . I mean . . . he just . . . all I said was yeah, I'd meet him there. I mean, I don't think he thought . . ."

To tell the truth, she wasn't exactly sure *what* Bradley thought.

"Um-hm." Graham eyed her knowingly. "Then those other two came in together. The ones with the obscenely outrageous testosterone levels."

"John and Ramone? Yeah, but . . . they . . . I mean . . . they can't think of it as a solo date, can they?" Lisa Marie stammered, embarrassed. She hadn't even remembered about Bradley when she was talking to John and Ramone. "I mean, they were together and we just said, yeah, we'd hang out at the prom. What's wrong with that?"

"Um-hm." Graham still wasn't buying it. "What about the luscious hunky one just now?"

"Who, Marco?"

Wait a minute. *Luscious? Hunky?* So that was it. Graham was jealous. Here he was lusting after half the guys she'd been flirting with, and then getting on *her* case for being too available! How hypocritical could a guy get?

"You're hot for him!" Lisa Marie laughed. She hadn't realized Graham was gay.

"Maybe," Graham admitted, "but I'm still right. Counting your not-so-little friend Marco, you've made four dates for the prom."

Lisa Marie replayed the scene with Marco in her head. Was it really a date?

He had come in with his hair all blown from riding the new Vespa his dad gave him for his birthday. Lisa Marie pointed out that he should have been wearing a helmet, and Marco had joked that as a congressman's son, he had "helmet immunity."

"It's like diplomatic immunity," Marco had said. "For heads."

It wasn't funny, but Marco had the kind of self-confidence that made everything he said seem cool and/or amusing.

"Lucky you," was the only thing Lisa Marie could think of to say. She was off her game today.

"So I hear you're going to meet up with John and Ramone at the prom," Marco had said, faking jealousy, which was obviously just his way of coming on to her. Marco couldn't *really* be jealous of *anyone*. He was so good-looking and such a player, he was never at a loss for girls.

"We're going to hang," Lisa Marie had said.

"What about me?" Marco had stuck out his mouth in a cute pout. "Don't I get any?"

God, he could be so brazen! But that's what made him sexy. Boldness was his strong suit.

"You can have your share," Lisa Marie had said, flirting back.

"Okay," Marco said, pointing a finger at her. "Remember—you promised."

She laughed. It was just a game, right? Just talk. He didn't think she meant anything much by it, she was pretty sure.

Lisa Marie felt Graham watching her closely.

"Okay, maybe I did say I'd meet four guys," Lisa Marie admitted. "But I doubt any of them thinks it's a real date."

"Um-hm." Graham went into the back room to refill the amaretto syrup.

As soon as he was gone, Lisa Marie took out a calculator that was under the counter. If she was going to meet four guys at the prom, she'd better look fabulous. How long was it going to take her to save up enough for that dress?

She did the math quickly and sighed. She'd been working at Starbucks for three weeks now, and didn't have quite half the money. And the prom was only three weeks away.

"Excuse me," a voice near the register said, clearing his throat for attention. "Am I wrong, or do you sell coffee here?"

Lisa Marie looked up and saw Li'l D standing there, giving her his best I'm-hot-and-you're-hot-so-what-are-we-waiting-for stare. His eyes were so deeply set, it was impossible not to be riveted by them.

"Hi. What can I get you?" Lisa Marie asked brightly.

"Make it a tall mocha," Li'l D said, staring at her intensely with his bad-boy grin. "I've got a sweet tooth tonight."

"One tall mocha blended coffee." Lisa Marie called it, just like she was supposed to. Only she didn't call it out loudly, since Graham wasn't there to hear. "It'll just be a sec."

"Hey, I'm ready whenever you are," he said in his low, sexy voice.

Lisa Marie laughed. Li'l D was so amazing—he just radiated self-assurance without strutting around like an asshole.

Still, a girl had to keep her defenses up.

"I'm guessing you're *always* ready," she said.

Li'l D tilted his head at her. "Hey, I can play by whatever rules you want to make," he said, sounding totally sincere.

He eyed her with such an intense look, she immediately felt tongue-tied and didn't know what to say. She stepped behind the coffee machine and started pouring the chocolate for his mocha.

"So what's this music?" Li'l D nodded up at the speakers mounted in the ceiling.

"Jazz mix. Starbucks's own blend," Lisa Marie answered. "The CDs are right there on the counter if you want to buy one."

Li'l D shook his head with a slow, disapproving smile. "They should stick to coffee."

True, Lisa Marie thought. But as a loyal Starbucks partner, she wasn't allowed to say so.

She poured hot coffee into the chocolate milk and stirred. "So is it true what everyone says—that you're getting a contract to record a CD?"

"It could happen," Li'l D said with a slight shrug. Like he didn't want to count his chickens, but there was a definite possibility. "I've been talking to some people. We're working on it."

He's the perfect guy, she thought. He had all the things she wanted. He wasn't all macho and full of himself—just cool enough to get his message across with smack-down power. His music was loud/angry/in-your-face, but his personality was laid-back/sensitive/quiet. What could be better than a guy who was sexy and hot and on the edge, but at the same time seemed like he'd let someone in if it were the right person—the right girl?

"You want extra whip?" she asked him.

"No whip," he said. "I forgot to say."

Lisa Marie heard him sort of humming while she finished making his drink. She wanted to look up, to see if he was watching her, but the espresso machine was so tall, she couldn't see over it.

Finally the coffee was ready. "One tall mocha blended coffee," she called, trying to make it sound like something she'd created just for him.

Li'l D's eyes were laughing when he took it from her.

"So do you have to stay back there the whole time you're at work?" he asked.

"Pretty much," she said. "Except when the tables need to be wiped or the milk and sugar bar needs to be refilled."

"The tables look damned dirty to me," he said, without turning around to look at them.

Lisa Marie laughed. "I just wiped them ten minutes ago. And besides, I'm alone right now. I can't leave the till."

Li'l D nodded and gave her another intense stare.

Then he grinned. "You . . . me . . . prom night." It wasn't a question.

"Definitely," Lisa Marie answered with a cautious laugh.

Her heart skipped a beat, excited. Was he serious? He'd definitely been flirting with her. But at the same time, she figured he was just playing around. Otherwise, why not come right out and ask her to the prom?

Li'l D grinned and left the store. On his way out, he turned to give her a two-finger salute.

"That's five," Graham said, coming up behind her from the back room.

"Oh, God! Do you think so?" Lisa Marie asked. "I mean, I don't think he was serious. Was he?"

She hoped so, but she really had no idea.

The look on Graham's face made her think, *Yeah. Maybe so.*

That would be incredible, Lisa Marie thought. Spending prom night with Li'l D was her idea of heaven. Of all the guys she'd been flirting with for the past few weeks, he was the only one who really made her heart go pitter-patter.

"Here comes number six," Graham said, nudging Lisa Marie and knocking her out of her daydream.

She looked up and saw Todd walking toward the counter like he wanted something other than coffee.

"That's not number six," she said under her breath to Graham. "That's my ex."

"Ooooh." Graham seemed intrigued. "Well, we're not busy, if you want to take a break."

Todd's face was all serious . . . and did she also detect . . . apologetic?

"Can I talk to you?" He pushed his straight black hair out of his eyes. He hardly ever cut his hair, and on some guys it would've looked cool. On Todd, it just looked forgetful.

Lisa Marie stepped out from the counter and stood in the corner, her arms crossed over her chest. "What?"

"I don't know." He was looking down at his feet, trying to pull it together to say whatever it was he'd come to say. "Maybe this isn't the right time . . . I just . . ."

"What? Just say it," Lisa Marie snapped. It was really awkward standing there in the corner, trying to have some kind of conversation with him while Graham pretended not to eavesdrop and stare.

She had no idea what Todd wanted, but whatever it was, she wasn't too interested in giving it to him. Why the hell should she? He had dumped her, unceremoniously, after two long, tedious years. What the hell was *that*?

"Okay." Todd met her eyes. "I was thinking . . . I mean, I wondered if you, maybe, wanted to try getting back together."

"Why?" She eyed him coldly.

Todd didn't flinch or look away. "I broke up with you because I wanted to ask Delia Apfelbaum to the prom," he said. "But she turned me down."

Lisa Marie had to smile. The one good thing she could always say about Todd was that he was a straight shooter, almost unnervingly honest. She didn't know any other guy who would just spit out the truth that way. It almost made her like him again. Almost, but not quite.

"Thanks for telling me the truth," she said softly. "But I've got other plans for the prom. I'm going with Marianna and Heather."

Todd looked hurt. He seemed to be racking his big brain, trying to think of some way to change her mind.

"I've got to get back," she said, turning toward the cash register.

"Okay. Well, maybe I'll see you at the prom?" Todd called hopefully. When she didn't answer, he slinked out of Starbucks, scraping his messenger bag on the doorframe on his way.

"I told you that was number six." Graham snickered.

Now you know how it feels, she thought as she watched Todd go.

Chapter 10

"It's our first date after dark!" Marianna bubbled with excitement as she waited with Heather in a neighborhood coffee shop for Luke to pick her up for date number three.

"I'm glad I don't have to go on this one," Heather joked. She hadn't actually *gone* on Marianna's other dates, but she'd driven her to and from them, so it almost felt like she had. "I get to leave when he picks you up, right? I've got so much studying for chem, it isn't even funny."

"You're studying on a Saturday night?"

"Don't even ask."

Heather had been hinting lately that she'd been too distracted to do much schoolwork, and Marianna knew exactly how she felt. How could she think about her classes these days? All her energy was channeled into two things: thinking about Luke, and trying to keep her dad from figuring out that she was dating on the sly.

Last week, she and Luke had had lunch at the mall and then went to his house for the big Ping-Pong playoff. Of course he beat her mercilessly, although there was a moment when she almost scored twice in a row because he was laughing so hard at her pitiful serve.

Heather had played chauffeur for that date, too, driving Marianna both ways. What else are best friends for?

But tonight was the real deal: dinner at a café with live music somewhere near Dupont Circle, which was Marianna's favorite trendy-yet-historic-shopping-and-dining D.C. neighborhood.

Heather was just keeping her company at the rendezvous point until Luke arrived.

"There he is," Marianna said, getting up. She had told Luke not to bother hunting for a parking spot. Why waste time they could spend together? "Thanks—talk to you later!" she called to Heather.

"Sure," Heather said. "I mean, call if you want. If it's not too late."

Funny, Marianna thought. If Lisa Marie had been there, she would have said, "Call me with all the details when you get home." For some reason, Heather didn't seem to want to hear about it if Luke got to second base.

She slid into the Volvo beside Luke and immediately smelled his aftershave. It was nice, so different from his sweaty smell in the mornings when they were running cross country.

"Kazanjian, you look amazing," Luke said, staring as she crossed her long legs.

"Thanks. You smell good."

"I hope you like Thai food," Luke said. "This place we're going has a bunch of different Asian things, but the Thai dishes are really awesome."

"Basil rolls it is," Marianna said happily.

When they got to the café, the place was empty and quiet—the music didn't start till later. Perfect, Marianna thought. This way they could camp out in the best corner booth, which was more like a tropical hut, draped with printed Thai silk fabrics and layered with red and purple spangled pillows. If the place had been crowded, they'd never have gotten such a prime location.

Luke ordered an appetizer sampler platter, and when it came, he ate the prawn pancakes expertly with chopsticks.

"I love watching you eat," he said between bites. "You're not like a lot of girls. They either won't eat, or won't admit they enjoy it."

"You should see me eat a lobster with my bare hands," Marianna said.

"With your bare hands?"

"My uncle Oscar taught me how to do it," Marianna said. "You can even get the meat out of the claws with nothing more than a dinner knife, if you know how."

"See what I mean? A girl who eats lobster with her bare hands!" Luke announced loudly to the neighboring tables.

Marianna giggled. She would have been embarrassed, but the nearby tables were empty, so no one noticed.

"Everything here is delicious," Marianna said, and meant it in more ways than one.

By the time the band started playing, it was ten o'clock. Marianna had promised herself that she wouldn't get nervous and start acting like she was going to turn into a pumpkin, but she couldn't help it. Even though she was theoretically having dinner with her friends at the mall, she knew her dad would grill her when she got home. How come you're so late? Doesn't the mall close at nine? Why didn't you eat earlier?

He'd want to make sure that they hadn't run into any opportunities to rub up against boys.

Just to spite him, she scooted closer to Luke. She turned her face up toward his. He bent his head and kissed her softly.

Mmm. His kisses were wonderful.

When she opened her eyes, he was looking at her questioningly. "What's wrong?" he asked.

"Nothing." It was a lie.

"You're worried about your dad?"

How did he know? He was amazing. He could even read her mind.

"Sort of."

"Let's go, then," Luke said.

He took her hand, and they walked to his car without saying anything. The spring night air felt soft on her face. She looked up through the trees on Connecticut Avenue and tried to find some stars, but there weren't any.

"I'll show you a good place to see stars," Luke said, pulling her closer to him while they walked to the car.

He turned on an oldies station in the car, and they drove for a while in silence. Even this part was nice, just riding in Luke's car, letting him decide where to go. He crossed the bridge over the Potomac and parked facing the river, just a few miles from her house.

"Come here," he said, pulling her toward him.

Making out with Luke in his car, with the cool night air blowing in the windows and the lights from the Jefferson Memorial sparkling across the way . . . Who needed to see stars, anyway?

Luke kissed her on the mouth, then the neck. Marianna thought she might melt.

He stopped before she was ready to. "I've got to get you home," he said.

Marianna fought the urge to say, "No, you don't."

When they reached her street, he stopped the car again, a few houses away, so her dad wouldn't see who was bringing her home.

"Listen," he said. "I've got to say this. I want to take you to the prom."

Wow. She'd been hoping he'd ask, even though she couldn't possibly say yes.

"I'd love to," she said, apologizing with her eyes, "but my

dad will never let me go with a date. I had to beg for two weeks—and Lisa Marie's parents had to call him three times!—before he'd even let me go to the prom with girlfriends."

"I figured," Luke said. "But I want to be there with you. Who cares if I don't pick you up? You can meet me there, and it'll still be a date."

"Yeah?" Marianna said, glowing.

"I'll even bring you a corsage," Luke promised, pulling her close for one last kiss.

Marianna floated from the car to her front door. She couldn't believe it! She had a date for the prom with the sweetest guy on earth.

Chapter 11

"We've got to hook her up," Marianna told Lisa Marie at lunch on Monday, while Heather was at the salad bar getting blue cheese dressing to put on the salad she'd brought from home.

"I know. I don't want to dump her the minute we get there, but . . ."

"Totally," Marianna agreed. "She needs someone to hang with. What about Derrick?"

"Oh, please. She can't stand him."

"How about Ahmad?"

"He's too short for her."

"Michael Frenkel?"

"Can't dance."

"Well, think! Who else is there? Although I admit it's going to be rough, since you've got half the senior class planning to meet *you.*"

Lisa Marie blushed but decided to ignore that one. "How about Tony? I still say it's Tony. She likes him."

"Who likes who?" Heather asked, coming back with her perfectly arranged salad of apples, walnuts, jicama, edamame, and gorgonzola on oak leaf lettuce.

"We're trying to think of someone for you to be with at the prom," Lisa Marie said almost defensively. "And I say Tony is the perfect guy."

"Not again." Heather rolled her eyes. "I thought we went over this."

"We did, and we agreed you're giving up too easily," Marianna said. "How about Max Snow? He's not going with anyone."

Heather sighed. "Honestly, you should give up on trying to find someone for me. You can both go off with your guys, and I'll be fine."

"Don't be silly. We'd never just abandon you. Come on, think. We made a list last week. Who was on it? Max Snow, Eric Sandberg, Tony . . . Oooh! I know! How about one of the Marshall twins?"

"How about both of them?" Heather joked.

"Whatever floats your boat," Marianna said with a shrug before she realized that Heather was totally kidding.

Come on, Heather, Marianna thought. *You're not even trying. It's one thing to be shy, but you've got to make at least* some *effort to get what you want in life.*

Heather took two bites of her salad. "Mmm," she said. "Extra blue cheese. I love when it's lumpy."

She was barely participating in this conversation. Marianna and Lisa Marie were having to work twice as hard.

"Tony's the best choice," Lisa Marie concluded. "He's not attached, and I *know* you like him. I saw you talking to him in the publications office last week."

"Really?" Marianna latched on to that piece of info real quick.

Okay, so maybe it was a little bit self-serving to be trying to hook Heather up for the prom, but she was doing it as a favor, too. Somebody had to help Heather get past whatever was keeping her from having a social life. "When was this?"

Heather was chewing.

"Come on—details," Marianna demanded.

"Umm, the lit mag people were working on the final issue last week, and I was doing layout for the yearbook," Heather explained. "Someone asked Tony to do a spot illustration for the mag . . . he didn't know what size to make it . . . I helped him figure it out. That's all."

"You were laughing and having a good time," Lisa Marie pointed out. "I saw you."

"He's funny," Heather admitted.

Lisa Marie and Marianna waited expectantly for her to elaborate. God, this was like pulling teeth.

"He's got a dry sense of humor," Heather explained. "Margo was asking everyone where to get a decent pair of jeans. Everyone knows she dresses kind of slutty, so Tony mutters, 'I'd have thought you'd want an indecent pair.' "

Marginally funny, but whatever.

"You had to be there," Heather said when neither of them laughed much.

"Well, so, talk to him some more," Lisa Marie encouraged. "He sounds perfect for you. Really."

Heather shrugged and got up to get more salad dressing.

The minute she was out of sight, Marianna reached across Lisa Marie and dug into Heather's purse.

"What are you doing?" Lisa Marie was shocked.

"I'm looking for her cell phone," Marianna said quickly. "I happen to know she's going to be in the pub office today after school . . . and I think Tony should be there, too."

She found the phone and dug the St. Claire's student directory out of her own backpack to look up Tony's number. Then she quickly sent Tony a text message from Heather. It said: "Meet me. Pub office. After school."

"Hurry. She's heading back here!" Lisa Marie warned.

Marianna slipped the phone back into Heather's purse just in time.

"Someone took all the chunks." Heather pouted at the dribble of blue cheese dressing on her salad plate.

Poor Heather. Why couldn't she get herself focused on what was important in life—like the prom? If she didn't work a little harder, she was going to end up spending the whole night alone.

Luckily, she had two good friends to handle the details for her.

"The sports section is a mess." Marty Alexander, the editor of the yearbook, leaned over Heather's shoulder in the pub office that afternoon and looked at the pages in front of her. Behind them, the yearbook staff was bustling around like crazy. The final sections of the book had to go to the printer in three days.

Heather had laid out the sports section in Quark and printed out PDFs of the pages. Now she had the printouts spread in front of her on a big table.

"Well, we can't start with lacrosse—it's too marginal," Heather argued. "That's why I put basketball up front."

"But if we start with basketball, it looks like we're sidelining the other sports," Marty explained. "Makes it look like we have a pecking order."

"We do," Heather said with a laugh. "Fess up. Why else did we put theater and dance in the front of the book, and all the sports in the back?"

"Because we hate the jocks?" Marty offered.

"*Hate*'s a strong word," Heather scolded.

"Yeah, you're right. More like utterly despise because we're intimidated by their big muscles," Marty said.

Heather laughed. "So what do you want me to do? You're the editor. It's your call."

Marty thought for a minute. "Put the cross-country team first," he decided. "Use a huge photo of Marianna. That way everyone will think you're just playing favorites with your friends, and the heat'll be off me."

"That's not fair."

"Cry me a river," Marty said. "It's my call, remember?"

He meant it, too.

Oh, whatever, Heather thought. She didn't really care about the sports section anyway, and it would be cool to use a big picture of Marianna.

She sat back down at the computer and started rearranging the pages.

"Hi," a voice behind her said.

Heather turned her head slightly, still staring at the monitor with one eye and clicking things with her mouse. Finally she looked up.

It was Tony. He hopped up onto the table beside her.

"Hi," she said absently, wondering what he was doing there. The lit mag had sent their stuff off to the printer a few days ago.

"I got your text message," Tony said. "Why did you want to see me?"

Text message? Heather shook her head slightly.

"I didn't send you one. You must be confused."

Tony reached into his tight black jeans and took out his cell phone. His all-black outfit—jeans, T-shirt, boots—set off his smooth, pale skin and blue eyes. Heather thought he looked like a postmodern painting.

"I'm not confused. This is your cell number, isn't it?" He showed her the text message.

Heather studied the phone and then saw what time the message was sent—during lunch that day.

Wow.

"My friends must have done that," she said, shaking her head in disbelief.

"Why?" he asked.

Good question, Heather thought. *How dare they?* She could only come up with one answer.

"They're trying to fix me up with you so they don't have to take care of me during the prom."

An approving grin spread across Tony's face. Was he charmed by her blunt honesty?

"So meet me there," he said with a shrug. "We can hang out."

"Really?" Heather hesitated. She didn't want a date—not with a guy. But Tony was nice, and he wasn't making it sound like a real date. Just friends. Plus having him lined up would at least mean that Marianna and Lisa Marie could give it a rest.

He shrugged again. "It'll be fun," he said casually.

"Okay."

Why not? She felt comfortable with him. Not all tense and nervous, the way she was around Katie. Maybe this could work out after all.

In fact, she was beginning to think that maybe she'd made a mistake. Maybe, if she gave guys a try . . . and if she just stuffed her feelings for girls . . . maybe her gay feelings would go away.

In any case, Tony was the lucky guy she was going to experiment on.

Chapter 12

"Why are we filling up on burgers and fries *before* we go dress shopping?" Lisa Marie asked as she took another big bite of her juicy Monterey burger, slathered in cheese and mushrooms. "I'm already bloated enough without this junk."

"No one made you order that!" Heather said. She sort of wanted to add, *And I wish you hadn't.*

The truth was, Heather was sort of repulsed by all the greasy food spread out on the table, but she didn't want to say anything. It was just one more way she felt different from her friends these days—and she didn't need that right now.

"We need fortification," Marianna said, encouraging Lisa Marie to eat without feeling guilty. "I ran 3K this morning. I'd never survive a shopping marathon without stoking up."

"Okay, but I want to go straight to BCBG as soon as we're

done," Lisa Marie announced. "I've been saving for forty-five days to buy that dress, and I'm taking it home today."

"What about shoes?" Heather asked.

"I've got enough for that pair of Jimmy Choo knockoffs," Lisa Marie said happily. "You won't believe where I got the extra money, either."

"Where?" Marianna asked, her mouth full of a Philly cheesesteak.

"Angela sent it to me." Lisa Marie was clearly pleased. "She said she had some cash stashed away for a rainy day, and she wanted my prom to be as perfect as hers was. Can you believe that?"

I wish I had a sister, Heather thought. Being an only child had its perks—she got just about everything she wanted or needed—but there was a downside, too. Like being too much the center of attention at home, especially now that her parents were divorced.

"That's cool about your sister," Heather said. "But what I meant about the shoes is that you're supposed to shop for them first thing in the day. Before your feet get all nasty and swollen. Otherwise, you'll buy a size too big."

"Really?"

"That's what I read," Heather said.

"I thought it was the other way around," Marianna argued. "Shop for shoes last. That way they'll still fit when your feet swell up."

"But then they'll be too big at the beginning of the evening," Heather argued. "We should do the shoes first."

"Oh, whatever," Lisa Marie said. "Let's just get the shoes over with so we can go directly to BCBG, okay?"

They finished eating, dumped their trash, hit the restroom, and then stopped in Sephora for a touch-up, to make sure their hair and lip gloss looked good.

As Lisa Marie put it, "We're going to be staring into mirrors; we'd better like what we see."

Then they made a beeline to Mar-vel-ous, Heather's favorite shoe store. They were known for carrying fabulous knockoff shoes at decent prices. Heather bought a pair of pointy green heels trimmed in velvet, and Lisa Marie got the black imitation Jimmy Choos.

Marianna tried on ten different pairs and then decided to wait until she found a dress. What a novel idea.

"So are we done here?" Lisa Marie asked. "Can I finally fulfill my dreams and aspirations, and blow five hundred dollars of my hard-earned cash on a killer dress that's going to make me look like the hottest chick at the prom?"

"Spend it, sweetie!" Marianna cheered.

BCBG was at the far end of the mall, a hike.

"You were right about getting shoes early," Lisa Marie said as they trudged through the crowds. "I've got blisters on my heels already."

They passed a group of four girls from St. Claire's, shopping bags in hand. Heather glanced and spotted Serena Moss's younger sister in the group.

I wonder if she's gay, too. Heather had been trying not to indulge in her favorite pastime, but she was addicted. Did lesbianism run in the family? she wondered.

It was a stupid question, and Heather knew it. When she thought about all the gays and lesbians she knew, or knew of, at St. Claire's, she could tell that gayness didn't run in the family. It wasn't predictable, either.

Lisa Marie made a diagonal turn and cut through a clump of guys from various urban D.C. schools, barely dodging a little kid with a dangerously sticky caramel apple in his hand. She was clearly determined to cut two seconds off their arrival time at BCBG.

Heather and Marianna followed her to the back of the store, where the black peau de soi silk dress was hanging on a peg on the wall.

"Oh my God, there's only one left," Lisa Marie gasped, grabbing the dress. "There were three here on Thursday!"

She fiddled with the size tag in the neckline, but it was folded back underneath, so she couldn't read it. Finally she found the price ticket and flipped it over.

"Oh, my God." Lisa Marie was hyperventilating. She spun around to the nearest salesclerk, a skinny dark-haired girl with a vapid expression on her face who was standing about twenty feet away. "Do you have this in a six?" Lisa Marie's voice carried halfway across the store.

It took forever for the salesclerk to move her butt over there, and Lisa Marie had to repeat the question five different ways. But the answer was still no. The dress was gone. They'd just sold the last size six about ten minutes ago. To another girl from St. Claire's.

Oh, boy. Heather could feel the tension in the air. Lisa Marie was clearly trying to control herself, trying not to blame anyone or throw a fit, but it was obviously a struggle.

"Can you get it? From another store?" Lisa Marie's voice was so shrill now that strangers were turning to stare.

"Sorry," the salesclerk said. "Can I show you something else?"

Heather took a deep breath. "It's so my fault. We should *never* have gone to look at shoes first," she said, feeling terrible. "I am so sorry. Oh my God, I really am."

"I've been saving for weeks! Killing myself at that job!" Lisa Marie moaned. She was still clutching the one remaining black dress as if it might somehow be made to work, but it was a size zero.

"I'm so sorry," Heather repeated. What else could she say? It wasn't *really* her fault that someone else bought the dress—not logically. Not technically. But it sure felt that way.

"Okay, this sucks," Marianna said, taking charge. "But calm down. Don't worry. We're going to help you find something better. I swear to God, we won't go home until we find you something Halle Berry would kill to wear to the Oscars."

The vibe in BCBG was too stressed for them to stay another minute, so Marianna wrapped her arm around Lisa Marie and led her out of the store. Calmly, she kicked into "personal shopper" mode and headed straight to a store that could soothe any girl's nerves: Stick, a boutique that carried the newest Stella McCartney.

All three of them tried on Stella McCartney dresses, mostly as a kick since they were outrageously expensive. When none of the McCartney dresses looked right on Lisa Marie, they prowled around some other racks.

"Here's something," Heather said, offering Lisa Marie a gorgeous lavender satin Marni gown.

Lisa Marie glanced, but shook her head. "I'm too short for that. Besides! It's $800."

True, Heather realized. *On both counts.*

For the next ten minutes, Heather and Marianna took turns bringing Lisa Marie dresses to consider, but nothing seemed right.

Then, all of a sudden, Lisa Marie spotted one she loved: a slinky black satin dress with a crossover halter neck and a low-cut V back. It was a designer they'd never heard of, though. The label said *Slic.* Like a cross between *chic* and *sleek*.

"So try it on," Heather said, draping the black dress over Lisa Marie's arm. "This could be the one."

They crammed into the dressing rooms with their arms full. Marianna had finally found what she wanted: a fabulous gown with a purpley-pink sequined top, narrow velvet sash belt, and full silver-bronze taffeta skirt—so hip/fifties it almost hurt.

Luke would love it, Heather thought. He seemed like the romantic type.

For herself, Heather took a white embroidered chiffon dress, just for a goof. No way would she spend $900 on a dress, and besides, she loved the green beaded flapper one she'd already bought. It was just a good way to kill twenty minutes, so she didn't have to hang around feeling like a wallflower.

There'd be plenty of time for that on prom night.

The dressing rooms were crowded, mostly with girls their age, or the next age bracket, which Heather's mom called HS plus ten—high school plus ten years, tops. Or women who were small enough to fake it.

"My boobs are spilling out," Lisa Marie called from her dressing room.

"Poor you," Marianna called back.

"No, really. This is too small." Lisa Marie's voice was getting tense and squeaky again.

Heather had slipped on the white embroidered thing, but it didn't work. White wasn't her color, except in the summer when she had a tan. This dress made her look like a flower girl at a suburban wedding.

"Let me see," Heather said, stepping into the hallway.

Lisa Marie came out modeling the black satin gown. She

was right—her boobs were spilling out the sides, near her underarms. The dress was way too tight.

"It's a six!" Lisa Marie complained. "Do I look like I've gained, like, twenty pounds or something?"

Heather knew better than to make a joke about the burgers and fries they'd just devoured. Instead, she turned Lisa Marie around so she could examine the inside label. Sure enough, the hangtag was wrong. The price tag said size six, but the inside label said it was a four.

"It's mislabeled," Heather said. "Hang on. I'll see if they have another one in your size."

It was awkward, walking back out into the store looking like an overgrown kid. Heather felt ugly in the dress, and she could tell people were watching her out of the corners of their eyes. Serena's little sister and her friends had come in, and they were fingering the cashmere sweaters up front. Lily Moss turned to whisper something to her friends.

Is she making fun of this dress? Heather wondered, feeling awkward and uncomfortable.

Heather hurried to the rack of black satin *Slic* gowns. There were only two left. A woman at least fifty years old was reaching for one of them, but Heather wasn't about to lose this fight. She lunged in front of the woman and grabbed both dresses at once.

"You're taking *both* of them?" the woman accused in an arch tone.

Heather checked the sizes. One was a six. The other was a fourteen.

"Here," she said, thrusting the fourteen back at the petite woman. "You can have this one."

Marianna and Lisa Marie were standing in the hallway of the dressing room, clearly eavesdropping on someone, when Heather got back.

Giggling, Marianna put a finger to her lips. "Listen." She nodded toward a dressing room a few doors away.

Heather followed Marianna's gaze. Behind the closed door, she could hear what sounded exactly like two girls making out. They weren't even trying to be quiet about it, either. One of them was moaning, "Oh, oh, oh yeah," and the other kept going, "Mmmm." It sounded like they were backed up against the door because someone kept bumping it.

Lisa Marie and Marianna were both laughing silently, their eyes wide open in totally scandalized shock.

"Who is it?" Marianna whispered.

Lisa Marie shrugged. "Someone having too much fun," she whispered with a laugh.

Heather was dying to know who it was, but she didn't want to act more interested than they were.

Still, a girl's gotta do what she's gotta do.

She bent down and looked under the door, trying to see if the legs gave any clue.

Nope.

Other than it was two white girls who had probably used Venus razors in the past three hours.

"Well, it's a free country," Marianna said, slipping back into her dressing room to change out of the sequin-bodiced gown. Lisa Marie took the size six dress and closed the door to try it on.

Clearly, they were done eavesdropping.

But Heather felt her pulse quicken a little as whoever was behind the bouncing door started moaning a little louder. Reluctantly, she returned to her own dressing room. Even if she couldn't hear the make-out session from there, she could still imagine it—and wonder who was behind those doors.

I feel like a freak, she thought. Why couldn't she just be herself? Be out?

One of these days, she was going to get up the nerve to let her friends know the truth. That she had a crush on Katie Morgan, and no desire whatsoever to spend the night with Tony at the prom.

Just the thought of prom night made her stomach tighten. It was going to be agony having to pretend . . .

Lisa Marie popped out of the dressing room in the black satin gown. It looked amazing on her.

"You're the best!" she said, throwing her arms around Heather, giving her a hug. She twirled for Heather's approval.

"Fabulous," Heather said, and meant it. The dress was so slinky and sexy, Lisa Marie was going to be a standout on prom night. And with that low-cut back, guys would go nuts.

There was so much skin showing, you knew she couldn't be wearing much of anything underneath.

"Prom is going to be the best night of our lives!" Lisa Marie announced, her face aglow.

Heather sincerely doubted it. But she didn't have the nerve to say so.

Chapter 13

Marianna's stomach felt fluttery as she pulled on a pair of stockings so sheer, she felt practically naked even when she was wearing them.

It's prom night! she thought, trying not to bounce off the walls with excitement. After waiting so long, and planning it for so many weeks, she'd been afraid that the real thing would be a letdown compared to her fantasies and anticipation.

Or worse, that her dad would do something to ruin the whole thing at the last minute—like telling her she couldn't go, or forcing her to wear a bulky sweater.

But so far, nothing bad had happened.

The whole day, in fact, had been a total buzz. She and Lisa Marie had hung out all morning at Heather's, talking about how great the prom was going to be, gossiping about which St. Claire's girls were likely to wind up with which guys by the time the night was over, and drinking green tea (Heather's idea) to calm their nerves while the three of them did their nails and gave themselves pedicures.

Then, on her way to the hair salon, Luke had called her cell three times because he was afraid the florist had messed up her corsage, and he was freaking that it wouldn't look right with her dress.

How sweet was that? Besides, Marianna didn't really care about the stupid corsage. Just having him care so much made her happier than anything with a straight pin and a fake piece of greenery ever could.

After lunch—fruit salad and toast that she barely picked at because she was too excited to eat—she lounged in a bubble bath and shaved her legs while listening to Ted Leo + Pharmacists on her iPod.

Now, with her hair perfect and her makeup so fabulous she was even looking forward to having her dad take a zillion photos, she slipped on her dress, stepped into her shoes, and went downstairs.

Okay, so maybe she was looking forward to *half* a zillion photos. What was it about her father that made him always go too far? The man knew no bounds.

"Just one more on the stairs, and that's all," Marianna's father said, clicking away on his digital Nikon D10. "Then we'll do a few on the porch."

"Daaaad." Marianna cocked her head to one side and let

her hair hang off her shoulders, because she knew it looked fabulous that way. But she put a sourpuss scowl on her face.

"What? You look beautiful," her father said, beaming at her. "And it's your first prom. We need pictures. Grandma will want to see them, too, you know."

Yeah. Well, they're going to be pretty weird pictures, Marianna thought. *Just one girl alone? In a prom dress? Without a date?*

Luke should be here. He should be in the photos.

Still, she didn't really mind that her dad was taking so many, because he was right—she did look amazing tonight. Barry, at the Aveda salon, had outdone himself with her hair, leaving some of it cascading at the sides and pulling some of it up off her face.

Her dress was unbelievable, too. It looked even more elegant now that she had the right jewelry—a retro black choker necklace.

"How about a few on the couch?" her father suggested. "Before we go outside."

Marianna shook her head. "I don't want to wrinkle my skirt."

"You'll wrinkle it in the car anyway," her father argued, pointing at the couch like she was a dog who would jump up and do tricks.

She sighed, but complied. The thing about her dad was that, no matter how obnoxious he could be with a camera in his hands, the pictures always came out great. Marianna thought he was probably a frustrated artist. Maybe if he'd gone into photography instead of wheeling and dealing in government contracts, he wouldn't be such a grumpy tyrant.

"I think Heather's here," her mother said, peering through the sidelights of their front door.

"Excellent," her father said. "I'll get some pictures of both of you."

Oh, great, Marianna thought. *Pictures of me and Heather—like we're a couple.*

I hope Grandma enjoys that.

By the time her dad was done posing them together on the steps, the porch, and in front of the big cherry tree in their front yard, Marianna wanted to strangle him. In ten minutes he'd managed to imply that Heather looked even more beautiful than Marianna did, treated Heather like she was "in charge" for the evening, and had flat out declared that Marianna's college choice was on the line if anything bad happened tonight.

"And you'd better have her home by twelve thirty," her dad warned Heather. "I mean it. Not a minute later."

Heather swallowed and shot Marianna a quick, questioning glance.

Was this torture ever going to end?

"We know, Dad," Marianna said. Twelve thirty was only half an hour after the prom officially ended. It was ridiculous, but what choice did she have? That was the best deal Lisa Marie's parents could negotiate with her father.

"Whatever you say, Mr. Kazanjian," Heather promised in her best good-girl voice.

As soon as they were out of the house, Marianna let out a sigh of relief. "Do you see why I was considering going to the University of Alaska?" she said.

"He's intense," Heather admitted.

"Well, anyway, you won't be stuck bringing me home at twelve thirty," Marianna said. "I'm pretty sure Luke will be driving me home."

She arranged her skirts in the front of Heather's car and checked the mirror. Her skin tingled, like it was just waiting to be touched.

This was going to be an unforgettable night, Marianna was sure of that. The only question was: Which part would be most memorable? The buildup had already been fantastic. Now it was on to Lisa Marie's, then dinner in an upscale restaurant in the hotel where the prom was being held, and then finally the prom itself.

Dinner would not be the most fabulous part, she decided. Who could eat at a time like this? But hey—it was part of the ritual, and she wasn't going to miss out on a scrap of it.

They pulled into Lisa Marie's driveway.

"Should I honk?" Heather said. "Maybe she'll just come out."

No such luck. Mrs. Santos was standing at the front door, camera in hand, waving them in.

More photos, this time with Lisa Marie in the middle.

More cautions about drinking and driving. Everyone assured Mrs. Santos it wouldn't be an issue because Heather was the designated driver, and she didn't even like to drink.

They parked in the garage at the Renaissance Hotel and rode the elevator up to the Florentine Restaurant, passing half the people they knew from St. Claire's Academy on the way. Marianna scanned the lobby, looking for Luke, but he wasn't there.

"Don't worry, he'll show up," Heather said reassuringly.

"Have you seen Tony yet?" Marianna asked.

Heather blew off the question. "It's not a date. We're just going to hang out if we feel like it."

Hopefully, you'll feel like it, Marianna thought. Otherwise, how was she going to get enough alone time with Luke?

Lisa Marie spotted John and Ramone in the lobby, dressed in identical rented tuxes, except that Ramone had gone for the hipper look—a silver necktie—while John was sporting a tacky red brocade vest and matching bow tie.

"Well, there are two of your dates," Marianna teased.

"Okay, don't start with me," Lisa Marie said.

"Oh, we're just getting started, aren't we, Heather?" Marianna laughed.

"Definitely," Heather agreed. "You've got five dates for tonight. You're never going to live that down."

"Do you have to go check in with them or something?" Marianna asked.

"It's not five dates!" Lisa Marie protested, but she was

glowing from head to foot. Marianna had the feeling Lisa Marie could barely contain her excitement.

Yeah. It was going to be a memorable night. That much was certain.

"I'm glad your mom took all those pictures of us," Marianna said. "Years from now, we'll be at some dreary high school reunion, probably in this very hotel, and we'll get out all those pictures and say, 'Can you believe we looked that hot on prom night?' "

The maître d' showed them to a good table near the bar. Being gorgeous, unattached young women didn't hurt when it came to getting decent tables. More than half the people in the Florentine were prom-goers, mostly couples and a few other groups of girls. But Marianna and her friends stood out in the crowd.

High school guys don't go out to dinner together, Marianna realized, glancing around. There wasn't a single group of prom guys in the restaurant.

Lisa Marie lifted her water glass to make a toast. "To us—and to having an awesome prom night," she said.

"Ummm," Heather chimed in. "To us."

"I already *know* I'm going to have an awesome night," Marianna said, thinking of Luke. "You're the one who has to choose between five guys, Lisa."

"Five? Or is it six?" Heather asked.

Lisa Marie stared. "Did I forget someone?" She was honestly not sure.

"Hello. *Todd?*"

"Oh, that. That's over," Lisa Marie said decisively.

Marianna ordered lobster tails and a salad. It was her night to indulge. Lisa Marie ordered two appetizers—shrimp spring rolls and the duck crepes—instead of a main course. Heather got the special—penne with broccoli rabe and pine nuts.

"So who do you really want to wind up with?" Heather asked Lisa Marie while they were nibbling pieces of crusty bread. "I mean, if you had to pick just one of your five guys?"

"You mean which one is likely to get to third base?" Lisa Marie asked.

Marianna laughed. "That's another way to put it."

"Okay, here it is. Bradley . . . nothing. He doesn't even get to bat. John . . . he's hot, but he's too full of himself, so first base, maybe, but just to see how it feels to kiss him. Ramone . . . he's more my type, really, but he's too stupid. I'd let him get to second base but only because I know he's too dumb to even brag about it."

Marianna shrieked with laughter. "You're outrageous!" she said.

"Tonight, I'm a cold bitch," Lisa Marie said.

Heather and Marianna both laughed. No way was Lisa Marie a bitch or a slut or anything like that—she was just playing the part and enjoying the limelight. What the hell. After two years with Todd, she was entitled.

"What about Marco and Li'l D?" Heather asked.

Lisa Marie pursed her lips, thinking. "Marco gets to second base if he treats me like royalty," she decided. "But that won't happen, because he's really a prick. A charming prick, but a prick."

Lisa Marie took a sip of her tonic and lime. Marianna could tell she wished it had gin in it.

"As for Li'l D . . . he's the one," Lisa Marie went on, more serious now. "But I don't think he's really into me."

"You never know," Marianna said. Poor Lisa Marie. Didn't she realize how great she was? Guys loved her sense of humor and the fact that she really knew how to kick back and have fun. For some reason, she didn't seem to get that.

"So Li'l D gets a grand slam?" Heather asked, probing for details.

Lisa Marie shook her head. "I'd love to make out with him, but I'm not having sex with anyone tonight. Doing it on prom night is tacky—unless you're really in love."

Yeah, Marianna thought, catching a meaningful glance from Lisa Marie. Was she in love with Luke?

"I'd settle for someone who would kiss me good night," Heather mumbled with a faraway look on her face.

Who's she thinking about? Marianna wondered. There could really be only one answer.

"That'll happen," Marianna reassured her with a nod. "Tony's your man. Just wait and see."

Heather blushed, and her head made an involuntary shake.

That proves it, Marianna thought. *She's so into him—she's afraid she'll get her heart broken.*

So leaving Heather alone with Tony all night would be a good thing.

Marianna felt much better now—now that she had a good excuse to dump Heather ten minutes into the prom, and go find Luke.

Not that anything would stop her.

Chapter 14

Heather stood at the edge of the dance floor in the hotel ballroom and scanned the glittery crowd. Overhead, the ceiling was draped with giant gold balloons and lamé black streamers—was this a theme?—while gold spotlights played on the walls, creating an unreal, vaguely glamorous effect. Word around school was that the prom committee couldn't agree about anything, so they'd given up. Someone had apparently ordered a bunch of cheesy stuff from some prom Internet site at the last minute.

Still, the mood was exciting, and there was some kind of buzz in the air. The dance floor was respectably full. It was still too early for a lot of the hippest kids to show up—that's why the place wasn't packed yet. But after a minute, Heather finally spotted the person she was looking for.

Katie. At least Katie was there.

Heather's heart pounded a little as she watched Katie dancing with the group of girls she'd arrived with. In her slinky beige gown cut on the bias, with tiny torn bits of netting sewn like trim along the seams and hem, she was a vision, a knockout. The tiniest pearl necklace hung around her beautiful long neck, and her golden hair fell everywhere, framing her shoulders and covering the thin straps of her dress.

No matter how crowded the dance floor got, Katie was the kind of girl people always made room for. There was this invisible cushion of space around her—as if she were the star of a movie, and the extras knew they had to leave room for the camera shot. You didn't crowd a girl like Katie Morgan. Her aura gave off a huge glow.

"Why aren't you dancing?" A voice beside Heather broke through her private space.

It was Marty Alexander, the yearbook editor, dressed like James Bond in a white dinner jacket, black bow tie, and black formal pants. Very East Coast preppy. Very old-school money. The dinner jacket didn't look rented, and it didn't look brand-new. Marty had done the formal thing before.

"Hi," Heather said, glad to have someone to talk to. She couldn't blame her friends for dumping her already—not really. She just wished they'd have spent a *few* more minutes with her before running off to be with their guy. Or guys. Plural, in Lisa Marie's case.

"You alone?" Marty asked, sounding surprised.

"No, I came with Marianna and Lisa Marie."

"So why aren't you dancing?"

The DJ was spinning something with a dance club beat, and Marty didn't seem to have anything more than a quick twirl on the floor in mind, so she let him take her hand and lead her into the crowd. The minute they hit the dance floor, she started to loosen up. Dancing was better than doing the wallflower act.

Marty grabbed her and spun her around to the right, then the left, throwing down some serious swing dance moves. He was pretty masterful, surprisingly so. Heather laughed, amazed at how people's personalities changed—some for better, some for worse—on the dance floor. Marty was suddenly a party animal. Who knew?

He spun her around again, and now she was back to facing Katie. Katie was bumping hips with Marco Wessington. Wasn't he one of Lisa Marie's dates?

When the song ended, Marty dipped her. So corny. Then he turned to leave.

Now what? Heather wondered, finding herself back on the sidelines again.

Suddenly someone turned the lights down even lower, and a mirrored disco ball began spinning slowly, scattering flickers of light all over the room.

A slow song came on the huge speakers.

"This is for all you lovers out there," the DJ said in his low, Al Green impersonation.

Through the crowd, Heather saw Marianna and Luke dancing close, lost in each other's eyes. It was obvious they were falling for each other—anyone could see that from a mile away.

Then she spotted Katie with her arms around Sarah McCallister's neck. Sarah had her arms around Katie's waist, and they were dancing the slow dance together.

For all you lovers out there? Oh, God. Heather's heart skipped a beat. Could it possibly be true—what she'd been hoping and wishing for? Could Katie possibly be gay?

Heather desperately wanted the answer to be yes, but she didn't want to hope too much.

She tried not to stare, but it was too riveting, seeing Katie in another girl's arms. Katie and Sarah's thighs were practically touching, although they were leaning back from each other, talking and giggling through the whole song.

It was hard to tell—was it just a goof?

Heather could feel herself getting all hot and aroused, just watching them.

I'm going to look like a freak if I don't stop staring, she scolded herself.

To make herself stop, she wandered along the edge of the dancing crowd. The slow dance ended, and more people pushed onto the dance floor.

Lisa Marie had to be here somewhere, didn't she? Yeah, there she was in a dark corner, kicking it up with John and Ramone, who were arguably two of the best dancers in the school. The minute Lisa Marie noticed, she waved Heather to join them.

Whatever, Heather thought, nodding and dancing on the fringes of their group.

Ramone ogled Heather, giving her his standard-issue grin. Her dress wasn't low-cut or revealing enough to push his buttons, and she knew it. She tried to smile back.

To be honest, Heather thought the music really sucked. In an effort to keep everyone happy, the DJ was bouncing from one kind of groove to another with no rhyme or reason, switching from techno to salsa to hip-hop to trance . . . it was insane. But at least she was at the prom. And she was dancing.

Where the hell was Tony, anyway?

When the song was over, she checked the time on her cell phone. Oh, Christ. It was only nine o'clock. Could she really take three more hours of this?

Marianna and Luke cut across the dance floor and dragged her out to join them.

"Where's Tony?" Marianna shouted over the blaring music.

Heather shrugged. "God only knows. Maybe he decided not to come."

Marianna shook her head. "He's just too cool to show up on time." She looked around, checking each group and scanning the corners of the ballroom to make sure. "His friends aren't here yet, either. They'll show."

"Whatever," Heather said.

Whatever. What was that? Her only vocabulary word for the night? Shape up, she told herself. All this self-pity was beginning to bore even her.

So what would she do if she actually did shape up?

All of a sudden, it hit her. She was living a sort of schizo prom night—attending two different proms, almost like two parallel realities.

There was the prom she was *supposed* to be doing: the prom where she and Tony hung out, danced, made small talk, and nothing happened, other than her managing to get through the evening somehow without blowing her cover and revealing she might be gay.

Then there was the prom she *wished* she could attend: the one where she and Katie danced all night, where she was out and honest about her feelings for girls, and where she let her heart hope for the things it was secretly hoping for.

But there weren't really two proms. There was only one, and this was it. This was her one and only chance to do senior prom right. Why was she blowing it so phenomenally?

She wandered through the ballroom, searching for Katie again, wondering who she'd be dancing with this time. But right then, the DJ took a break, and everyone sort of split up. Katie headed for the restroom.

What the hell, Heather thought. *You only live once.*

She took a deep breath and decided to follow her.

Chapter 15

The restroom was down a long carpeted hallway in a quieter wing of the hotel, just out of the way enough to make Heather feel slightly like a stalker, but at the same time, private enough to give her the impression she and Katie were alone.

The heavy, dark mahogany door with *Ladies* etched in a shiny brass plate swung shut before Heather reached it, so she had to push it open again after Katie went in.

There she stood at the long mirror, glowing even more in the soft restroom lighting, surrounded by the scroll-and-gilt-edged mirror, golden sconces, and marbled everything. She was leaning forward slightly to look at a jeweled clip in her hair. Something was tightly clutched in her left hand.

Heather took only a few steps into the room, then froze. She didn't need to pee. She didn't need to comb her hair or fix her lip gloss or check for spinach in her teeth. She had come for only one reason . . . to see how it would feel to be this close to Katie Morgan on prom night.

"Hi." Katie smiled as their eyes met in the mirror.

Heather's heart picked up speed. They were alone, she was pretty sure about that. Or at least, the stalls were quiet, and it seemed like the place was empty. Her pulse quickened in a way she hadn't felt since The Moment in New York when Serena Moss put her arm around Heather's shoulders.

Only this was better. Because this was Katie. This was what prom night was all about—standing behind the most beautiful girl she'd ever seen. The one. Alone together.

"Hi," Heather said, frozen still.

Katie turned slightly and opened her hand to show Heather what she was holding. It was the delicate pearl necklace—the tiniest strand of perfect little beads Heather had ever seen. "My necklace came undone," Katie said. "Can you fix it?"

"Sure." Oh my God, was this really happening? Was she really alone with Katie Morgan, helping her put her necklace back on? The sounds of music and prom-goers and laughter just barely filtered through the thick door. It seemed like everything outside that bathroom was just a dream.

"It's a tricky clasp," Katie said, turning back to face the mirror so that Heather could hook the necklace from behind.

Heather's hands were almost trembling. She reached around Katie's neck and grasped the two ends of the necklace, one piece in each hand. Her breath felt shallow. Her mouth was so close to Katie's hair. She felt so light-headed, she could barely keep her eyes focused on the reflection of the necklace in the mirror . . .

"Oops."

The strand of pearls slipped from Heather's left hand and dangled down into the cleavage of Katie's dress.

Katie giggled, her eyes still locked on Heather's in the mirror. She didn't move, she didn't even flinch. What did she expect Heather to do? Get it?

Okay. If that's what she wanted . . .

Heather reached forward, toward Katie's plunging neckline. Her arm brushed Katie's shoulder, and Heather felt her own face glow with a kind of heat that made her feel like she might pass out. The end of the necklace dangled just half an inch below the ragged lace edging. With two careful fingers, Heather reached to retrieve it.

Her hand was right at the top of Katie's dress when the restroom door opened and Emily VanDerMoot walked in.

"Katie, where the hell . . ." Emily stopped in her tracks. "Oh. Major lesbo moment."

Katie laughed lightly, not the least bit embarrassed, and she still didn't flinch.

"Heather's just fixing my necklace," she said, smiling.

Heather's face flushed bright red as she fumbled with the damned thing, hooking it as quickly as she could. Why did they have to make those clasps so impossibly tiny?

And why didn't this hotel have more restrooms? So certain people could be left alone when they wanted to be?

Katie turned around to face Heather. "Thanks," she said, and for just an instant Heather caught what she thought was a meaningful look behind her smile.

Or was it?

Was she ever ever ever going to learn how to read the signals?

"Listen, you *can't* just disappear like that," Emily was saying, grabbing Katie by the arm. "Jessie's freaking because her cell phone died, and she missed a call from Nat, who was supposed to be bringing . . ."

Their voices faded as they disappeared back into the hallway, back toward the prom. The restroom door closed gently behind them.

Heather stood there on the marble-tiled floor, feeling completely confused. She stared at herself in the mirror. What was she supposed to do? Did Katie mean something with that parting glance? Was she interested in Heather . . . or just trying to be friendly? When, if ever, would Heather know how to act . . . how to respond . . . how to *be* a lesbian?

It was just too much trouble, Heather decided. Too hard, too crazy, and it made her feel like too much of a loser.

She fluffed her hair, fixed her stockings, and decided for what felt like the billionth time to put all this misery behind her.

It was time to go hook up with Tony.

Chapter 16

"Have you seen Heather?" Marianna was still moving with the music, tossing her hair around and boogying to match Luke's amazing dance moves. She and Luke had somehow worked their way across the dance floor and wound up near Lisa Marie and her cluster of guys. It gave Marianna a chance to multitask.

Lisa Marie was surrounded by John, Marco, and Bradley, although she appeared to be mostly dancing with John, if body language was any clue. Marco and Bradley were just hanging on the edge.

Lisa Marie shook her head. "Not in a while," she shouted above the music.

Oh, well. She's probably fine, Marianna thought, laughing

at a wild hip-gyrating move Luke was trying out, probably for the first time.

Marianna couldn't believe her luck. Luke was such an amazing dancer. Every move he made was interesting or expressive. It was almost theatrical, the way he threw himself into wild, exaggerated moves that looked like they could have been choreographed by someone doing a music video. But it wasn't a "look at me" type of dancing. More like, "who cares who's watching?"

Luke spun around and struck an angular pose on each hit of the reggae music.

Marianna laughed and tried to imitate him.

"You okay?" she called to Lisa Marie on one of the spins.

Lisa Marie beamed. "Fabulous!"

"Me, too," Marianna said, glowing with total happiness.

What could be better than this? Prom night . . . Luke . . . her dress and the corsage he'd brought her . . . her friends nearby . . .

She never wanted it to end.

The DJ segued into a slow song, and Luke pulled her close. She wrapped her arms around his neck and rested her cheek on his shoulder. Their hipbones were almost touching.

"We should have been doing this all year," he whispered in her ear.

Ummmm. She wanted to stay in his arms all night . . . forever . . .

When the slow song ended, Luke took her hand and nodded toward the exit. "Let's get something to drink."

Marianna followed him happily. She was dying of thirst—they'd been dancing forever.

She thought he would head for the refreshment table the prom committee had set up, with soft drinks in plastic cups and platters of finger foods, but he passed it by. Instead, he led her to the elevator in the lobby. "Brad has a keg in his car," he explained, pushing the down button.

Even the elevator ride was a turn-on. Alone in a cozy space . . .

She nestled close to him, and they both spontaneously looked up at the mirrored ceiling, their eyes meeting at the same time. It made them laugh.

Too bad the door opened so soon. Marianna thought he'd been about to kiss her, but just then they arrived at the parking garage.

In the dimly lit garage, a couple of other St. Claire's guys were standing at the back of a Ford Explorer a few rows down, just about to close the hatch.

"Leave it open," Luke called.

The guys left the rear door up and strolled past Luke and Marianna with red plastic cups in their hands.

"Hey, Perchik," one of them said.

"Hey, Perchik's chick," the other said.

Luke and the guys laughed, and Marianna glowed more. Was it true? Was she Luke's official girlfriend?

He squeezed her hand. "Feels good to get away from the noise for a while," he said.

When they reached the car, he let go of her hand and drew off two cups of beer into red plastic cups. "They match the prom committee's cups, so we can take them upstairs," he said.

"Clever." Marianna took a drink and closed her eyes. The cold beer felt wonderful on her hot, parched throat.

"Yeah," Luke said. "Brad's idea."

"Bradley Boulter? He's with Lisa Marie tonight."

"No. Brad Morganthal."

Oh, right. Morganthal was on the cross-country team.

"Have I mentioned you look amazing?" Luke said, pulling her close to him with one arm. He bent his head slightly, and Marianna lifted her face instinctively for the kiss. She closed her eyes as she felt his soft lips on hers. This was better than the beer. When Luke pulled back, his eyes were dancing. "Want to spend the night in the Lincoln Bedroom?" he asked.

Marianna's eyes popped open wide. The Lincoln Bedroom . . . at the *White House*? Could he possibly be serious? She knew a few girls who had gone to the White House for parties with the president's daughters. But how on earth . . .

"You're kidding, right?" she said.

A grin spread across Luke's face, and he nodded toward a long black Lincoln Town Car parked a few spaces away. "Right there. Dave Smethurst rented it and dubbed it the

Lincoln Bedroom. A bunch of us chipped in. I think it's occupied right now, though."

Marianna glanced and saw the back of a white prom dress on someone who wasn't exactly sitting up straight. She couldn't see much through the windows, though—they were tinted pretty dark.

"Looks busy in there," she said.

"Yeah. We'll come back later," Luke said.

She smiled up at him, and he pulled her close for another long kiss, this one more passionate. Marianna felt lightheaded. She'd been waiting a long time to feel these things. To be kissed like that . . .

It was definitely not a letdown.

She put one hand on the back of Luke's head, wishing she didn't have a beer in her other hand. Wishing she could just spend the rest of the prom right there in the parking garage.

She'd danced enough already, shown off her dress and her shoes and her guy to enough people, gotten enough compliments to last a while. Now all she wanted was some alone time with Luke, making out, getting lost in his arms.

She hadn't really decided how far she'd let him go—that wasn't something you planned in advance, was it? But there was one thing she was sure about: She wouldn't go all the way. She wasn't ready for that yet.

Luke kissed her cheek and then took her hand, leading her back into the hotel.

What time was it, anyway? Marianna wondered. She had

already calculated that it was eleven minutes from the hotel to her house. That left nineteen minutes to fool around after the prom ended. Assuming they stayed for the whole thing . . .

Luke looked down at the cymbidium orchid corsage he had pinned to the strap of her dress.

"Oops. Sorry. I think I crushed your flower," he said.

"That's okay," Marianna said. "Crush it all you want."

Chapter 17

"I thought you were here with me," Bradley shouted as Lisa Marie rocked out on the dance floor.

What? She couldn't really hear him. And to be honest, she didn't exactly care what he was saying. She was having more fun than a girl had the right to expect on prom night.

Who wouldn't want to dance in her shoes? Although she had to admit, the Jimmy Choo knockoffs were beginning to hurt. She was surrounded by five gorgeous guys, all of them vying for her attention, bringing her drinks when she took a break (she loved rum and Coke, thank you, Marco, for carrying that flask in your jacket), and making her feel like the queen of the prom. For all the other girls who were there with just one guy Lisa Marie felt nothing but pity.

Bradley mouthed some words again, this time pointing to

Lisa Marie, and then to himself. "Can we dance one of these alone?"

Okay—so there was a downside to having five dates. Bradley was becoming a pest. Lisa Marie made a face, pretending she couldn't hear him over the music, and turned her back. She found herself dancing face-to-face with the one guy she could see going solo with. The one who knew how to push all her buttons . . . all the good buttons, anyway.

Li'l D was wearing a black tux with a black shirt that was open at the neck—no tie. His dreadlocks were pulled back and tied behind his head, making his architectural cheekbones even more noticeable.

"Hey, baby," Li'l D said. He eyed her black satin dress. "Nice gown."

Lisa Marie smiled, and Li'l D returned the smile with a barely perceptible nod. Everything about him was minimalist and cool. He hardly moved when he danced, but he moved enough so you could tell he was feeling it—feeling the music, feeling her. It worked.

"Yeah," Li'l D nodded approvingly. "You are by far the best-dressed bitch at the ball."

Lisa Marie laughed, loving the way he talked. He had this uber-cool street cred/attitude thing going on, but at the same time, it was obvious there was a lot more to him.

Li'l D moved closer, close enough so that their bodies bumped every once in a while. His eyes drilled into hers, like he was seeing her soul and simultaneously exploring every intimate crevice of her body and brain. Lisa Marie had to admit that when he looked at her that way, she had a change of heart: Maybe it wasn't better to be there with five different guys. If she and Li'l D could spend some time alone getting to know each other, just talking . . .

She twirled and caught a glimpse of Bradley, who was glaring at her from the edge of the dance floor. What's his problem? Did he really think she was going to dump all these other guys and just hang with him?

Oh, Christ. Now Ramone was staring at her, too, looking pissed off.

Screw it, Lisa Marie thought. She didn't owe them anything. They'd *all* been playing with her at Starbucks—she knew that without a doubt. If she'd taken any one of them too seriously, she'd be the one getting burned.

Besides, the word around school was that Ramone was trying to get back with Tara, his ex. So let him.

Lisa Marie let herself go with the music, bumping and grinding when she turned her back on Li'l D, then pressing up against him when they were face-to-face. Then a slow song came on the sound system. She waited, wondering if Li'l D would take her in his arms, but he didn't. He just kept moving to the music, close to her, drilling her with his intense eyes.

That's okay, too, she thought, matching his mood, slowing down, moving the way he did. There was something even sexier about dancing so slow and close, without touching.

Was this the best night of her life? Duh.

A lot of people had left the dance floor, ready for a break, or a drink, or whatever. They were probably headed upstairs, she decided. Some of the wealthier kids had rented hotel suites for the night, for after-parties, even though it was technically against school rules. From what John had said, she figured she'd be going up to one of the parties, too—but not yet. She had no desire to leave the dance while Li'l D was still there.

Just as Li'l D reached out to put both his arms around her waist, the crowd thinned a little, and Lisa Marie caught a glimpse of Todd standing on the other side of the room.

He was just standing there all alone, staring at her.

How long had he been doing that? It creeped her out a little bit. Not because he could ever be a stalker or anything. He just looked so lonely . . .

For a minute she felt a pang of guilt. Poor guy. All alone at the prom, couldn't get a date . . . Except . . . why should she feel guilty? *You dumped me, remember?*

As soon as Todd caught her eye, he headed toward her, making a beeline straight through the dancers.

Oh, no. Not now. Please . . . don't spoil this moment. Was he actually going to cut in?

Yup.

He tapped Li'l D on the shoulder. "Do you mind?" he said.

Li'l D didn't say a word. He simply backed off without an argument, putting his hands in the air as if to say, *She's all yours*. But he gave Lisa Marie a sexy wink right before he turned away.

"What?" Lisa Marie asked, putting her left hand on Todd's shoulder and her right hand in his palm. At least she wasn't going to dance close with him or let him wrap his arms around her possessively in front of the whole school.

"What's wrong? You can't even stand to dance with me now?" Todd sounded like a hurt puppy.

"Look—you broke up with me," Lisa Marie snapped. "So I'm just not sure what you're doing."

"I told you I wanted to get back together," Todd said, waltzing her gracefully around the floor.

Weird, Lisa Marie thought. She hadn't realized Todd knew how to waltz. Or that he was such a smooth dancer. Was this the first time they'd ever slow-danced together? It couldn't be. She tried to think back, but the rum and Coke had made her head feel kind of fuzzy.

"Sorry, Todd," she said. "But I'm here with a lot of friends."

And I don't want you spoiling my night or making anyone think we're back together, because we're not!

But she didn't have to say that last part—he got the message. When the song ended a moment later, he just said, "Thanks," and walked away.

One thing you could say for the guy: He wasn't dumb.

Chapter 18

As Heather walked back into the ballroom, the DJ turned on the disco ball again, and the sparkling light began flashing everywhere, like little bits of mirrored confetti raining down on the prom.

Where was Tony, anyway? she wondered. It was getting late. If they were going to hang out, they'd better hook up soon.

By now, some of the black streamers had fallen from the ceiling and were littering the floor. Fewer people were dancing, although the floor was still crowded enough so that you couldn't see straight across it. Clumps of people had spilled out into the lobby, where they were lounging, kicking off their shoes and stripping off their ties, or just hanging out in the halls outside the ballroom.

The prom's almost over, Heather thought. And she still hadn't had enough fun, drama, or memorable experiences to fill a diary page.

If she was going to make this one count, she had to get busy.

She headed for the refreshment table, deliberately taking a wide path around Katie and her friends who were huddled off to the side, talking on someone's speakerphone cell, trying to solve the big crisis, whatever it was.

"Hey!" Lisa Marie came up to Heather at the refreshment table and squeezed her arm. "Having fun? Where's Tony?"

"I haven't seen him yet."

"Oh, wow." Lisa Marie searched the crowd herself. "I saw him a few minutes ago . . ."

Well, at least he's here, Heather thought. She was afraid maybe he was going to be a no-show.

"Don't worry about me. I'll bump into him sooner or later," Heather said.

And if she didn't? She'd have to cope. There were plenty of other guys out there she could experiment with. Marty Alexander, for one. She could feel him eyeing her every time she passed the group of guys he was hanging with.

"Are you sure you're okay?" Lisa Marie asked, clearly worried that Heather was having a bad time.

God. This was the last thing she needed—Lisa Marie pitying her.

"I'm good," Heather said. "How's it going with the gang of five?"

"It rocks!" Lisa Marie said. "I've been dancing with Li'l D for like, forever, but I promised Marco the next slow one, so I've got to go. You *sure* you're okay?"

"For the third time, yes! Get out of here and quit cramping my style," Heather joked, shooing Lisa Marie away.

With a small cup of club soda in her hands, she wandered through the lobby, then back into the ballroom, searching for Tony. He had to be here somewhere . . .

Just looking for him made her feel better. It was such a relief to stop thinking about Katie for a while. She didn't even want to think about *not* thinking about her. She just wished the whole topic would go away.

Finally she spotted Tony in a dark corner of the main ballroom. He looked amazing, she had to admit. He was wearing an elegant designer tux with the palest pink shirt she'd ever seen, and a long, sleek, black necktie. His wavy hair fell down over his forehead just enough to give him a hip bed-head look.

There was only one problem: Was that a video camera in his hands?

Heather made her way to him just as he turned the camera on and started shooting a bunch of people who were holding a private conversation in the corner.

"Hey," she said, not quite sure if he was in the middle of something.

Tony didn't answer and didn't flinch, but after a longish pause he swung the camera in her direction. The red light on the front indicated that he was still shooting.

"Hi, stranger," she said, looking right into the lens, giving him a little smile.

Tony kept shooting, but he moved the camera away from his face and gave her a warm smile back. "Hi. What's up?"

"Nothing. I just thought we were going to hang out," Heather said. "You want to dance?"

"Sorry," Tony said. "I got here late. And I can't dance now—I've got this going on."

He pointed at the camera with his free hand.

"Well, could you turn it off?" Heather asked bluntly.

"Sorry, that's not happening," Tony said. "I'm making a documentary about the prom." He eyed her dress, taking in the shoes, the bag, everything. "You look fantastic, by the way."

Heather relaxed. Was that the first compliment she'd gotten all evening? It felt like it. "Thanks." At least that was something.

"So what's the documentary for?" she asked him.

"I got into NYU," he explained. "They have an incredible film school that can seriously launch your career. I'm shooting a bunch of footage for an independent project I want to do over the next few years."

"That's so cool," Heather said.

"So how's the prom?" Tony asked, sounding more like a documentary filmmaker than a cute guy chatting her up.

"Eh," Heather shrugged. "It's okay. So are you . . . I

mean . . . are you going to be doing this video thing all night?"

"Not *all* night," he said, grinning at her and sort of mocking her at the same time. Then he put the camera back up to his eye and zoomed the lens in close. "But right now, I want to interview you." He made it sound like a come-on.

Okay, Heather thought. *This could be fun.* At least she still looked fabulous—that much was true. Everyone else was pretty rank by now, they'd been dancing so long and partying so hard. The good thing about not having a date was that she still looked fresh at eleven P.M.

"So what do you think of the prom theme?" Tony asked, kicking into interviewer mode.

"What theme?" Heather said. "Did someone forget it's not Halloween?"

Tony laughed, like that was exactly the kind of answer he was hoping for. But she couldn't tell if he actually agreed with her, or just liked having someone being snotty about the decorations on tape.

Was this an interview . . . or a date?

"How would you rate the DJ?" Tony went on. "On a scale of one to ten . . ."

"Ten being you want to kill him and steal his record collection? And one being you want to kill yourself if you have to listen to another minute of this crap?" she said.

Tony laughed. "Yeah, something like that."

"I'd give him about a three," she said honestly. "I mean, he's kind of schizo, bouncing from one kind of beat to another. I mean, seriously, do you like this stuff?"

A kind of Latin beat dance thing was playing right then, and Tony shrugged. "With the right partner," he said, giving her a sly smile.

Well, then, why don't we dance! Heather wanted to say. But she didn't want to sound whiny.

"Okay, so tell me, Heather Proule, what prom night means to you," Tony said, sounding all serious and deep and personal, like he really cared about her answer. "I mean, what do you hope will happen tonight?"

He moved the camera away from his face—although it was still taping—and gave her an intense pierce-your-heart, open-your-soul stare.

"I don't know." It was a lie, but she wasn't about to spill her guts on videotape. With her luck, the movie would probably go straight to Sundance. She could see the posters now: *Prom Night Pathos, A Film About Loss and Rejection,* by Tony Vilanch.

Besides, right at that moment, she had no idea what the truth was.

Did she want Katie? Or was she really hoping she could forget her feelings for girls and find out how it would feel to be with a guy?

"No, honestly, tell me," Tony said. "Is prom night different from every other night of the year? Would you do things tonight that you wouldn't do at any other time?"

"Like what?" She was stalling. Trying to hide the thoughts that were racing through her head.

"Like sex," Tony said, cocking his head.

Whoa. Was he coming on to her? Or did he ask everyone this stuff?

Just then Emily VanDerMoot came up and poked her head into the frame, interrupting. Right into the camera, her face close to Heather's, she said, "Tell him about your major lesbo moment in the bathroom."

Then she walked away.

Oh my God, Heather thought. *Thanks a lot, Emily. Why don't you just out me in front of the whole school?*

Tony raised an eyebrow. "Really? This is interesting. Tell me more."

Heather's heart was pounding. She didn't want to talk about it at all—and certainly not on video! Her head raced, trying to think of some way to change the subject.

"Come on," Tony said. "Let's hear about that."

Heather felt trapped.

"Why?" She blurted out the first nervous comeback she could think of. "Do you want to make it a threesome?"

Wait a minute—that didn't sound right. And from the look on Tony's face, she wasn't sure he knew she was just kidding.

Tony grinned at her with his Cheshire cat smile as the camera light continued to blink red.

Oh, man. He's going to win a freaking Oscar for this. And I'm going to be the laughingstock of the D.C. private school brat packs.

Suddenly Heather wanted to disappear, as far away from him as she could possibly get.

"I've got to go," she said, turning around and walking away.

Great exit line. Write that down, Heather. Be sure to use it again real soon.

Chapter 19

"I'm starved," Marianna said as she and Luke rode the elevator up from the parking garage. She had skipped breakfast and lunch so that she'd fit into her dress without the slightest hint of a tummy bulge, and had pecked at her lobster tails, too nervous and excited to eat. Now she was on the verge of a major blood sugar drop. Her stomach was growling, and she prayed Luke wouldn't notice. "I could kill for some blueberry pancakes."

"You total cow," Luke teased. "I saw you and Lisa Marie in the Florentine. You were scarfing down an entire side of beef. Each."

"We were not!" Marianna shrieked, punching him. But of course his outrageousness just made her like him all the more. How many guys could get away with calling a girl a cow, even as a joke, without being instantly strangled or stabbed with a stiletto heel? "I barely ate at dinner. Can we grab something? I'll even eat dried-up, crusty old chip dip if there's any left on the refreshment table."

Luke gave her hand a squeeze. "I can do better than that." He sounded like he knew a secret. "Stick with me."

When the elevator reached the lobby, Marianna started to leave, but Luke pulled her back. Then he pushed a button that took them back down to a subbasement level. The door opened onto a deserted hallway with cement walls and floors. It was clearly not part of the public space in the hotel.

"Where are we going?"

"You'll see." With a mysterious smile, he led her through the empty corridor to a set of double swinging doors. Beyond them was another hallway, which angled off and led past the huge laundry room. It looked like hundreds of towels and sheets were being washed.

"Are we allowed to be here?" Marianna felt like a trespasser as they prowled deeper and deeper through the underground corridors of the hotel.

Luke stopped and pulled her close to him as he leaned against the concrete wall. "No one's here," he said. "Who will know?"

She closed her eyes and let him hold her tight against his body. The smell of beer on his jacket reminded her of the long, passionate kiss they'd shared in the garage. The whole prom was all wrapped up in that one kiss, it seemed to her.

Suddenly a door opened and a uniformed hotel waiter came bustling past them, pushing a room service cart.

Uh-oh. Marianna flinched. Too many years of her father's strict rules. She hated getting in trouble.

"Luke! Whatchoo doin' here?" The waiter grinned, smiling as he passed.

"Hey, Francisco." Luke nodded to the waiter. "Prom night."

Francisco kept moving, like he didn't have time to stop. "Keep it real with the pretty lady, Luke-o!" he called as he disappeared around a corner. "And say hey to Danny for me!"

Marianna was stunned. "You know him?"

"My brother Danny used to work here last summer," Luke explained. "As a bellhop. He showed me all these back corridors and underground tunnels that lead to the kitchens and stuff. Come on."

He took her hand and led her to another service elevator, kissing her again when the doors closed. *What a night,* Marianna thought. It felt magical, being in all these private, secret places with Luke. Every time they were alone for a minute, he kissed her again, or she kissed him, and time seemed to stand still.

Finally the elevator opened onto a short hallway that lead to the main catering kitchen. The place was bustling with a crew of about five cooks and sous-chefs still whipping up food for twenty-four-hour room service. Luke poked his head in the door and waited for someone to notice.

"Lukie," the main chef called, nodding when he caught sight of them. "Hey! How's my favorite little bellhop's brother?"

Luke slapped high fives with the chef, whose name was Vigo. Then he introduced Marianna.

"She's got a craving for blueberry pancakes," Luke said. "Got any leftovers lying around?"

Vigo raised an eyebrow. "Cravings? Don't tell me . . ." He gave them a scolding leer and stared at Marianna's belly, like he thought she might be pregnant. Then he burst out laughing. "Just kidding, Lukie! Blueberry pancakes? No problem. You guys sit right there."

Vigo pointed to a single tall metal stool in the corner and got to work making blueberry pancakes, hot off the griddle.

"You know the head chef?" Marianna whispered, impressed.

"I hung out here a lot last summer," Luke said. "Vigo used to make omelettes for me and Danny late at night."

Luke lifted Marianna up onto the seat and stood facing her, his hands still on her waist, leaning his forehead against hers while they waited.

Who needs food? Marianna thought, although her stomach was still rumbling like an old beater car. Just being with Luke, looking into his eyes, kissing him—all the special moments they were sharing.

What was a little hunger, anyway? She could always eat tomorrow.

Vigo brought a plate of blueberry pancakes, perfectly arranged, with a piece of orange peel and a sliced strawberry garnish on the side.

"Thank you so much," Marianna said.

"Anything for Lukie's lady," Vigo said with a bow. "You want syrup?"

She shook her head. "I like them plain."

"Enjoy," Vigo said as he went back to work.

Luke kept his hands around her waist while she ate.

"Can I have a bite?" he asked, opening his mouth to be fed.

She fed him a bite of pancakes, then took one herself.

Blueberry pancakes were her new favorite food. She'd never forget this moment as long as she lived.

In the elevator back up to the hotel lobby, he kissed her again, and this time the kiss lasted forever. They were still going at it when the door opened.

"Hey, get a room," someone joked from the crowd of kids who were waiting for the elevator to take them to the parking garage.

"Don't worry," Luke whispered to her. "I already did."

"Really?" Marianna wasn't so sure she was ready for that. On the one hand, she had been thinking about the Lincoln Bedroom on and off for the past hour, hoping they'd get a turn before the night was over. But still . . . did he really think he could just get a hotel room for the two of them without asking her first?

She looked at him questioningly.

Luke laughed at the expression on her face. "Not a private room," he said. He was searching through the crowds in the lobby for someone, she wasn't sure who. "A bunch of guys . . ."

Before he could finish, someone tapped him on the shoulder. It was Evan, a tall, skinny guy with an intellectual face. Marianna didn't really know him, but he was one of Luke's friends.

"Get your butt up to 1657," Evan said. "The party's about to start."

"After-party," Luke explained to Marianna. "We all chipped in on a suite."

A suite? Suite meant more than one room. Maybe she and Luke could spend some time alone in one of the bedrooms . . . if there was more than one.

This was weird, she thought. Two seconds ago, she was dragging her heels about going upstairs. Now she was trying to maneuver him into one of the bedrooms before it was too late.

Okay, so she was like just about every other privileged private school kid. She wanted whatever she couldn't have. So what else was new?

"Luke! Upstairs!" someone else called, pointing.

Marianna glanced at a big grandfather clock standing in the lobby. It was just about to strike midnight. Pumpkin hour. She was supposed to be home in exactly thirty-one minutes. If she was even a few minutes late, her dad would get nuclear.

Luke still had her hand, and he was moving back toward

the bank of elevators again. Marianna hadn't told him about her curfew yet—and now didn't seem like the time. Not until she checked out the party, anyway.

Maybe her dad would buy it if she told him that she really really tried to get home on time, but Heather was nowhere to be found?

Yeah. Right.

But who cared? This was her one and only senior prom, and the after-party was where it all happened. She wasn't going to miss out on any of it.

They pushed into the crowded elevator, which was jammed with at least ten other people, mostly prom-goers, including Bradley and Marco, two of Lisa Marie's "dates."

Whatever happened to Lisa Marie, anyway? Marianna wondered.

Maybe when they got to the suite, Marianna would call her cell, and check in. After that, she and Luke could cuddle on a sofa, or somewhere else . . .

The smell of beer and whiskey filled the stuffy elevator and prickled Marianna's nose. Yeah—they weren't the only ones who had started early.

"This is going to be an awesome party, dude," someone standing next to Luke said. "Have you seen the suite yet?"

"No," Luke said. "We haven't been up there yet."

Half the people in the elevator got off on the sixteenth floor and followed Luke and Marianna down the hallway to a room at the end.

Wow. How many people were invited to this party, anyway? She hoped it wasn't *too* crowded. Nothing like a loud, drunken crowd to kill a romantic mood . . .

"I hope I'm lucky tonight," Luke said as he pushed open the door to the suite.

"Well . . ." Marianna started to say.

But as the door opened, she caught a glimpse of a big round table set up in the middle of the living room, covered in green felt and poker chips. John was sitting in a prime seat, shuffling cards. About twenty-five people were crowded around, jammed into every corner of the suite.

Lucky? She thought he meant . . .

But no.

John waved them into the room.

"Okay, gentlemen!" John announced. "Open your wallets. The poker game is about to begin."

Chapter 20

"Poker?" Marianna took in the scene, trying to figure out whether Luke knew about this in advance.

The suite wasn't as big as she'd hoped, although it was nicely decorated in colorful, modern furnishings. But people were jammed everywhere—standing in the small entryway near the minifridge, lounging all over the chairs and sofas in the living room, crammed into the little hallway that led off to the bedroom and bathroom on the side. She and Luke had to squeeze through the crowd to even get into the room, pushing past couples who were already making out, or sharing a cigarette, or just getting wasted on tiny little bottles of Jack Daniel's from the minibar.

"It's a tradition," Luke explained, still holding her hand as he tried to find a seat at the poker table. "A bunch of seniors started it a few years ago—prom night poker. John said we've gotta carry it on."

John had shoved the coffee table aside to make room for his portable poker table, and someone had brought extra chairs up from the ballroom downstairs. You could barely walk, with all the extra furniture.

"Are you going to play?"

"Get your butt over here, Perchick!" Uri called.

Luke didn't answer either of them, but he let go of Marianna's hand and took a seat at the table.

O-kay. Not quite the scenario she had in mind, but it was pretty cool anyway, she decided. Now that Luke was there, the table was almost full. Uri, Evan, Vlad, John, Ramone, and Marco had all taken their jackets off and were throwing out money to buy stacks of chips. A bunch of people—mostly singles—were hanging around the edges, perched on the sofas or standing to watch.

This is like a movie, Marianna thought, feeling excited. Like Monte Carlo or some decadent L.A. Oscar night party. The guys looked amazing in their tuxes, and they were playing their roles to the hilt. John started passing around cigars, and spewing out all kinds of poker terms like *flop* and *river* and *kickers*.

Marco tossed a huge wad of money on the table, just to show off.

"Oooh, high roller," some girl mocked him.

"Big wad, small balls," someone else cracked.

"You want to try them?" Marco shot back.

The room was too noisy for Marianna's taste, but there was something crazy and thrilling about the atmosphere. Everyone seemed to be in the mood to take a risk. Two girls and two guys she hardly knew were playing beer blow in a corner, laughing hysterically every time they saw an ace. At the rate they were chugging beers, they were going to be trashed in about five minutes.

So what was she supposed to do? Hang over Luke's shoulder like something out of *Pretty Woman* and bring him luck?

Okay . . . she could do that.

"Hey, stranger." Lisa Marie came out of the bathroom and gave Marianna a quick hug.

"Hi!" It felt like forever since she'd seen Lisa Marie. "Are you okay?"

Lisa Marie nodded. "Is this an unbelievable night or what?"

"Totally." Marianna wished they could grab a little privacy. She wanted to tell Lisa Marie about the blueberry pancakes and the Lincoln Bedroom and how deeply she was starting to feel about Luke, but not with that geek Tom Zappato leering and listening to every word they said.

She pulled Lisa Marie back into the bathroom and closed the door.

"So what do you think of Luke?" Marianna asked Lisa Marie.

"What do *you* think? Isn't that more the point?" Lisa Marie said.

"I'm so into him." She couldn't hide the truth.

"Yeah. You look it. You guys were missing half the night." She smiled and raised one eyebrow. "Anything I should know?"

Marianna shook her head. This still wasn't private enough. Details about what an amazing kisser he was would have to wait. She couldn't do it justice with two people pounding on the bathroom door to get in.

"Tell me about your night. What's it like having five hot guys as dates?" she asked.

"It's a little tricky, but I'm handling it," Lisa Marie said. "I kinda wish it was just one person, though."

"Drew?"

Lisa Marie nodded.

"I saw him out there." Marianna nodded toward the living room.

"Yeah, with his arms wrapped around Sara-frigging-Franklin!" She looked pissed.

Marianna didn't know what to say. What did Lisa Marie expect, when she was "handling" five guys at once?

"I think he was just talking to her," Marianna offered.

Someone pounded on the door again. *Shit.*

"We'd better get out of here," Marianna said.

"Okay." Lisa Marie glanced at her wrist, but she wasn't wearing a watch. "Hey, have you seen . . ."

"Heather!" Marianna realized it at the same time. "Not in hours. We should call her."

"Open up, or I'm going to pee on the rug!" a girl's voice cried from outside.

Marianna opened the door and Tara, Ramone's ex-girlfriend, burst in. She was ready to lose it.

"Knock yourself out," Lisa Marie said, leaving and closing the door behind her.

Marianna stepped into the bedroom, which for some reason was the least crowded spot. Only about four people were hanging out, drinking, chatting, and watching the Game Show channel.

She pulled out her cell phone and saw that she'd missed four text messages. Even with her cell set to ring loud, she hadn't heard it once.

She dialed Heather's cell. "Where are you?"

"Where the hell are *you*? I've been looking everywhere." Heather sounded slightly upset. "I promised your dad to have you home on time—remember?"

Her dad? Marianna had forgotten all about him. Hah!

"Screw it, I'm not leaving now," Marianna said. "Come upstairs. We're in a suite, a bunch of people are having a party and playing poker." She turned to someone nearby. "What room is this?" she asked.

"Room 1657."

"Okay. See you in a few," Heather said and clicked off.

Marianna made her way back to the living room. The poker table was full—a few girls had joined the game—but she found a spot on the edge of a sofa arm and sat by Luke's side. He handed her a glass of Red Bull and vodka and she took a big swig.

If Daddy could only see me now, she thought with a mixture of guilt and pride.

That's what a good dose of Red Bull and vodka will do for a girl.

Chapter 21

"Burn that card, Uri, I've got some action going, and I don't care if Evan did just cripple the deck."

John was babbling nonstop, slinging poker lingo right and left, when Lisa Marie came out of the bathroom. He called out to her the instant he caught her eye.

"Hey, where'd you go? I need you here for good luck."

"Ignore him." Ramone motioned for Lisa Marie to come over to his side of the table instead.

John patted a seat right behind his chair. "No, no. She's my lucky charm for this hand; I'm feeling it."

"You're going to need *some* kind of luck, the way you've been losing tonight," Vlad needled John.

"Oh, shut up and deal the river card," one of the girls at the table said.

Lisa Marie grabbed another bottle of beer—what was this, her fifth? sixth?—and went to sit behind John, since that was the only seat open. She passed behind Ramone's chair on the way.

Was this really happening? Were guys fighting over her now? She couldn't help smiling inside, although she knew better than to let her happiness show.

She put a bored expression on her face and tossed her hair back over her shoulders. It tickled the skin on her bare back.

Okay, I still look hot, she thought, remembering how amazing she looked in the slinky black dress. Maybe if she sat there with her back to Li'l D, acting cool, playing the part of John's and Ramone's lucky bitch, Li'l D would get jealous and notice. Maybe then he'd want to talk to her.

All it would take was one look from him, and she'd gladly dump the other four . . .

"Awww, you're killing me," Ramone complained when she didn't sit on his side of the table. He was drunker than he had been the last time Lisa Marie danced with him an hour ago. She was a little more buzzed, too.

"Play nice. There's enough of me to go around," she said, trying to calm things down.

"Woo-hoo," Marco snapped sarcastically. "You think?"

Ouch. There was something decidedly cruel in his tone, but Lisa Marie couldn't think of a snappy retort. She sat silent, watching the hand play out.

"All right! The river hit me!" John yelled. "Okay, baby! We won!"

John turned and tried to kiss her on the cheek but pretty much missed. She was sitting farther away than he thought.

"Oh, for God's sake, keep it down," Rebecca called from the corner of the room. "You're not on *Celebrity Poker Showdown*, you know."

As John raked in a pile of money, Ramone threw his cards across the table, hard.

"You gave away my hand, didn't you?" he said, staring at Lisa Marie.

"What?" Was he insane? That was a terrible thing to say.

"You told him what I had. You saw my cards." He repeated the accusation loudly.

"You're an asshole, Ramone," Lisa Marie snapped. "You probably would've lost with five aces and ten queens."

Suddenly everyone was quiet, except for the TV blaring in the bedroom. Lisa Marie could feel the tension in the room.

"Chill, Ramone," Luke said. "You got a bad hand, that's all."

"Yeah," someone else said. "Don't bet with your dick next time."

Several guys snickered, and then someone said derisively, "Ten queens?"

Oh, please—did they *really* think she didn't know there weren't ten queens in a deck? Fine. Let them think what they wanted. Raising her voice had raised the stakes, and it worked. Ramone was obviously pissed, but at least he backed down.

"Jesus, I was only kidding," he said. "Can't you take a joke?"

Liar. Whatever.

She started to get up to get some air, but John grabbed her around the waist and pulled her onto his lap.

"I told you, you were my lucky charm," John said in her ear.

Then, right in front of everyone, he started trying to make out with her. He stuck his tongue in her mouth, and his hands were all over her. With everyone watching! What did he think—she was part of his winnings, or something? What a jerk.

Lisa Marie pushed him away as hard as she could, and struggled to stand up—but it was a major effort. She had fallen into his lap at a funny angle. Plus, did Jimmy Choo have any freaking idea how it felt to walk in high heels?

"God!" Lisa Marie said when she caught her balance and managed to get out of John's lap.

She stomped off, but it was a small suite, and there weren't many places to go.

What a crazy night, she thought, pretending she needed to use the bathroom again. Actually, coming to think of it, she did need to go. Anyway, standing in line at the locked bathroom door gave her something to do.

Her head was starting to throb a little, right at the temples.

Had Li'l D seen all that? And if he did, what did he think? She was hoping he'd get jealous or intrigued or competitive or something when Ramone and John were fighting over her—but of course he was too cool for that. And anyway, he seemed to have disappeared.

Just as long as he didn't think she was acting like a slut. It was so hard pulling this group-date-hang-with-five-guys thing off. Great concept—sucky reality. When she danced and flirted and hung out with all five of them at once, she felt a little bit like a tramp. And when she ignored some of them to be with just one guy at a time, the others sulked and acted like she was cheating on them.

Okay, now she *really* had to pee.

She knocked on the bathroom door. "There's a line out here," she called to whoever was in there.

"Out in a sec," a muffled girl's voice said.

Tara came up behind her and got on line. "Hey, there's your boyfriend," Tara said, nodding toward someone who had just walked into the suite.

Lisa Marie turned toward the door and saw Todd standing there, alone, gazing around the room. His hair was still combed, his shirt still tucked in, his jacket still fresh.

She looked away the minute he glanced in her direction, and didn't look back. She could feel him staring at her. Finally, out of the corner of her eye, she saw him leave.

Good riddance, she thought. She had enough men on her plate for one night. As much as she didn't want to hurt Todd, she didn't want to deal with him either.

She pounded on the bathroom door again.

"Minute!" someone called.

Well, hurry up, for God's sake! Lisa Marie thought. The real problem with standing in line for the bathroom was that you couldn't escape when someone like Bradley—who was walking toward her right now—tried to corner you.

Oh, please, Bradley, don't make this hard on me.

"Hey, you want to get out of here?" Bradley asked.

"Um, no thanks," Lisa Marie said.

He shot her a glare, as if to say, *What kind of bitch just turns a guy down flat?* Couldn't she at least make up an excuse?

Nope. Not right now, she couldn't.

Finally the bathroom door opened, and Marianna came out.

"Oh, it was you!" Lisa Marie was surprised. Weird. She had been ready to be all annoyed at whoever was hogging the bathroom.

"You okay?" Marianna asked.

"Ummm. Headache. And I've gotta pee. And Drew still hasn't tried to talk to me, although we danced together half the night."

"Go talk to him," Marianna said. "Seize the day!"

"Go use the bathroom first," Tara said, "or let somebody else go."

Lisa Marie slipped into the bathroom and out again as quickly as she could. Which meant she took five minutes to fix her makeup and try the complimentary little bottle of hand cream that was tucked into a basket on the vanity.

Now what? Marianna had gone back to sit at Luke's side at the poker game, which was getting louder and louder. A lot of people had migrated into the bedroom, probably sick of the posing and showing off at the poker game.

John, Marco, and Ramone were still into it hard-core, and from the looks of things, it wasn't going to end anytime soon.

Lisa Marie was tired of that. She grabbed another beer and looked around for Li'l D. Had he already gone?

No . . .

He was in the bedroom, still talking to Sara Frigging Franklin.

She should change her name, Lisa Marie thought. Yeah. Sara Frigging Franklin—it would make a good monogram. Two *F*s, with the *S* in the middle. Or was the *F* supposed to go in the middle? But then it would be SFF—like her initials. That wasn't right. Oh, whatever, she didn't care. Her head hurt too much to think straight . . . but Sara should change her name anyway. She was sure about that.

Suddenly, Lisa Marie felt a wave of sadness wash over her. She stared at Li'l D and Sara, totally baffled. What had happened tonight? Had she blown a chance to really be with him? How come he had danced with her so much, and it had been so special and magical and sexy, and now he didn't even seem to know she was alive?

As if he could feel her energy, he looked up right then, and their eyes met. He had been in the middle of a sentence, but when he caught her eye he just stopped talking to Sara and stared at her.

Okay, maybe he did know she was alive.

Wouldn't it be amazing if he actually liked her? She could just picture the two of them—they'd be the hippest couple in St. Claire's graduating class. They'd be partying at hip-hop clubs all summer, hanging out after his music gigs, maybe she'd even get to sit in the control room when he recorded his first CD.

Go talk to him, she told herself. *Go now. While you have the chance. He's staring at you for a reason. Isn't he?*

Yeah—there had to be a reason. Lisa Marie just wasn't sure what it was.

Was he wishing she'd come over and hang with him so he could get away from Sara Frigging Franklin? Or was he thinking, *Ew. Scary stalker girl. Let me out of here?*

That was the trouble. She didn't know. And she wasn't about to risk being totally, humiliatingly rejected in front of a room full of people, no matter how drunk and unlikely to remember it in the morning they were.

Chapter 22

"Are you just going to stand there staring at him?" a voice behind Lisa Marie said.

She whirled around and found Heather standing behind her, looking as fresh and beautiful and perfect as she had six hours ago.

"Hey, you! We were worried about you! Where have you been all night?" Lisa Marie was glad to have someone to talk to. Gaping at Li'l D was getting her nowhere.

"Around." Heather shrugged, like there was a lot she wasn't saying but didn't intend to go into it here. She changed the subject. "It's late. Don't I have to get Marianna home?"

"Did you ask her? Let's get out of here so we can talk." Lisa Marie nodded toward the door of the suite.

They grabbed Marianna away from Luke, and the three of them headed into the hallway outside.

At least the air was clear out there—clearish, anyway, if you didn't count the fake-clean smell the housekeeping staff sprayed all over the place—and the thick carpet made it seem pleasantly quiet.

"You having fun?" Marianna asked Heather.

"Sometimes," Heather said with a strange smile. "Listen, it's almost twelve thirty. What about your dad? We've got to leave right now if we're going to get you home."

"Screw Daddy!" Marianna declared with a slightly drunken slur.

Lisa Marie laughed. "Yeah. Screw Daddy!" she agreed.

"Are you sure?" Heather asked.

Marianna bit her lip slightly. "I don't know. I mean, my dad'll kill me if I'm late . . . but who cares? This is my senior prom, and I'm never going to get to do any of this again."

"You could say you're spending the night with me," Lisa Marie offered.

"Perfect!" Marianna jumped at the idea. "Yeah. That's what I'll do. I'll call him and tell him I'm going to your house."

"And don't even mention my curfew," Lisa Marie suggested as she fiddled with strands of hair that were falling down. "He doesn't need to know I'm staying out till two."

"Right. Although the mood I'm in, I feel like telling him your curfew is four!"

"Not so smart," Lisa Marie cautioned her.

Marianna's father was a piece of work. Even compared to the macho fathers Lisa Marie had grown up around in Venezuela, Mr. Kazanjian somehow seemed worse. Maybe because he was so infuriatingly calm while successfully controlling Marianna's every move. It creeped her out.

Inside the suite, a loud cheer erupted from the poker table.

"I'm going back in," Marianna said. "Maybe Luke lost."

"You sound like you hope so!" Heather was shocked.

"I wish he'd either win or lose so we could get out of here," Marianna said. She opened the door and slipped back inside.

Heather followed, and Lisa Marie was right behind her. From the looks of it, the poker game was nowhere near over.

Fine, Lisa Marie thought. That gave her a second chance to screw up her courage and go talk to Li'l D. But first she needed another drink—to bolster her resolve. She found an open bottle of vodka and poured herself a shot. Okay, two shots. Glass in hand, she snaked her way through the suite, past the bathroom, looking for him.

The bedroom was crowded, but Li'l D would be hard to miss.

She didn't see him anywhere.

Was he gone? But how was that possible? He couldn't have left without her noticing—could he?

Unsteady on her fake Jimmy Choos, she stumbled back into the living room and looked for a place to sit down.

Marco glanced up right then, a big cigar in his mouth, and smiled.

"Come. Sit." He patted his lap. "I've got a good hand, and you'll bring me luck."

Why were these boys treating her like she was some kind of carnival prize? She didn't like the way they were passing her around from one guy to another, and she definitely didn't want Li'l D to see her that way. But then again, if Li'l D was gone, how much could it really matter? Marco was hot. And he was smooth—he knew all the gentlemanly moves that made a girl feel like going along with his game.

Besides, she'd look like a tease if she didn't keep her word and spend some time with each of the guys on prom night.

"Okay."

"Seven!" Luke shouted when someone dealt a card. "Oh, man."

It was intense. These guys were so into winning. Lisa Marie could feel the testosterone level in the room throbbing and pulsating, like some kind of sci-fi beast.

Or was that the buzz from the vodka?

She squeezed past John's chair to reach Marco, who made room for her on his lap. Hmm. He was hot, but not in the sexy way. In the warm-body-temperature way.

He put his arm around her waist and leaned forward so his face brushed her hair.

"I'm all in," Marco said, pushing all his chips toward the center of the table with his free hand.

"Whoa." Luke's eyes opened wide. "That's bold. I'm out."

Lisa Marie was a little too bleary to follow the game. But whatever *all in* meant, she had the feeling this was a big deal. The table got quieter for a moment.

Vlad dealt the last card, and everyone bet some more. Uri was taking his time, like he couldn't decide what to do.

Slowly, almost imperceptibly, she felt Marco's hand start to slide from her waist and work its way down. But it was one of those did-he-mean-to-move-it kind of deals. His hand slipped so little, she wasn't sure whether he was being fresh or just getting tired. It inched down to her hips . . . then her ass . . .

So lame, and yet so effective. It was classic groper technique. When guys did it right, you couldn't tell whether they were trying to feel you up or not—so you let them get away with a lot more. It was like *you'd* be rude if you said anything.

Oh, whatever, Lisa Marie thought. Once his hand landed on her ass, it didn't seem to be going anywhere. Besides, it felt kind of cozy.

Her head was buzzing. What happened to that drink?

"So what have you got?" Vlad asked, eyeing Marco.

"Full house!" Marco flipped over his cards and raked in the pot. He leaned close to her ear again, reeking of cigar smoke. "I knew you'd bring me luck."

Lisa Marie turned to look straight into his eyes. Was anyone home? Or was that sultry, sexy voice just part of his game?

Cannot predict now, Lisa Marie decided. *Outlook not so good.* In any case, he didn't make eye contact.

She started to get up, but Marco grabbed her waist. "No way. Stay. You're helping me win."

Wouldn't it be great if that were true? she thought hazily.

She tried to pay attention as the next hand was dealt, but she was tired. Maybe she needed something to eat, or . . . No. What she really needed was another drink to keep her going.

Just then, the bathroom door opened, and Li'l D walked out.

Her heart skipped a beat. So he hadn't left! Well, okay. That was good news. Funny how her energy level could shift gears all of a sudden when something good happened.

She watched him as he went toward the bedroom. He seemed to be looking for someone who wasn't there. Then he turned back to the living room, and their eyes locked again.

Was he looking for her? Could he possibly be?

And here she was, sitting on Marco's lap.

Li'l D threw her an unreadable, smirky smile. She couldn't tell what it was about, but something told her to get out of Marco's lap—now.

She jumped up.

"No, wait," Marco said. "You're my luck, remember?"

"Get your own luck," Lisa Marie said, trying to squeeze her way out from behind the poker table.

The furniture was so tightly pushed together, she was sort

of trapped. She had to climb up on the coffee table to get out. Whoa. It was high up there. She felt a little dizzy. Maybe you weren't supposed to mix vodka and beer all in one night?

"Okay, gentlemen, let's see what you've got," Evan said shoving some chips into the pot.

"Pocket rockets!" Vlad announced.

"Pair of tens."

"Flush. Read 'em and weep, gentlemen."

"Shit!" Marco yelled. "I'm cashed out. Damn it, Lisa Marie, it's your fault."

Lisa Marie looked over at him. *My fault?* Was he out of his mind? What was it with these guys, always trying to blame her? But there was no point in arguing with him. Or slapping him down. He was just venting.

All she wanted to do was move this stupid chair, so she could go talk to Li'l D. But the damn thing was stuck, and she couldn't push it enough to even get past it. Oh, what the hell. She put her foot on the upholstery and hoped the fake Jimmy Choos wouldn't poke a hole.

Now where did he go? By the time she'd extricated herself from the furniture jungle, Li'l D seemed to be gone.

No. Not quite gone. He had his hand on the door, and he was about to leave.

"Wait," Lisa Marie blurted out, hurrying over to him.

Li'l D glanced over his shoulder without turning fully around. "What's happening, baby?"

"I just . . ." She didn't know what to say. She just wanted a chance to talk to him, really. But how could she say that?

She flashed on what he had said to her in Starbucks. Could she make this come out the right way? "Uh . . . you . . . me . . . prom night. Remember?" she said.

"You've been pretty busy," Li'l D said.

Was that an accusation, a compliment, or a complaint?

"A girl likes to keep moving," Lisa Marie said. "I'll sit down when the music stops."

Li'l D laughed. "Don't look like the music's going to stop anytime soon," he said glancing back at the poker table.

"Gamblers always lose," Lisa Marie shot back, not even sure what she meant by that, but hoping it sounded right. It was something her sister Angela had always said.

He cocked his head at her. "That's right," he nodded sincerely. "That's why I didn't sit down with those jerks. They're just throwing good money away."

Wow. It was sort of a shocker, hearing St. Claire's number-one hip-hop artist coming off more straitlaced than the congressman's son.

Li'l D took her face in one hand, very gently. "You . . . me . . . next time . . ." he said in a very sexy but sincere voice.

Then he and his buddies, who'd been hovering right behind her the whole time, were out the door.

So all right, Lisa Marie thought. Next time! Those were words a girl could hang on to.

She felt light-headed, but not from the alcohol this time. Drew liked her. She could tell. There was going to be a next time.

As far as she was concerned, her prom night was complete. She didn't care what happened next.

Chapter 23

"Is that your cell ringing and ringing?" Marianna asked Heather.

Heather looked down at the tiny little green and gold evening bag that was lying beside her on the sofa in the hotel suite. Was it ringing? It was hard to tell, with all the noise of the endless poker game, the music playing in one room, and the TV droning on in the other. (And by the way: What was it about being stoned out of your mind that made the Game Show Network so fascinating, anyway?)

If her phone was ringing at this hour on prom night, with her two best friends right there in the room, it could only be one person: her mom. She quickly snatched it open.

Wrong. The number displayed in caller ID wasn't anyone she knew.

"Hello?" Heather decided to answer it.

"Heather? It's Tony."

"Oh! Hi. Uh . . ." *How'd you get my number?* she wanted to say, but it seemed kind of rude and pointless.

Tony seemed to guess the question. "I had your number in my cell from the other day," he said. "From when your friends texted me from your phone."

Heather liked people who anticipated and explained.

"Anyway," Tony went on, "I'm getting out of here to a party at Nick's house . . . and I know we were supposed to hang tonight . . . so do you want to come?"

"Nick?"

"Nick Peron. He's a friend of mine. He lives in Chevy Chase."

Chevy Chase, Maryland, was one of, if not the, most desirable suburbs in D.C., filled with beautiful, sprawling old houses and wealthy political types who couldn't bear to be more than fifteen minutes from Capitol Hill. Mentioning it was code for *You're going to like his house, and you'll be driving in a safe neighborhood.*

"Um, sure. Can I bring my friends, if they want to come?"

"Yeah, I guess so."

"Okay. Where is it?" Heather asked.

"Meet me in the lobby," Tony said.

This was an excellent turn of events, Heather decided. She had thought Tony was blowing her off altogether, and that she'd go home from her big senior prom completely empty-handed—which is to say, with nothing more than a pathetic story for her journal about how she got all hot and bothered when an amazing girl needed her necklace fixed.

She'd also been positive Tony thought she was a jerk after she walked out of his video interview.

Maybe she and Tony could hook up after all—she was still willing to give it a try. And if not, at the very least, she could make nice to him so he wouldn't use the embarrassing parts of the interview in his prom night documentary.

She checked in with Marianna and Lisa Marie to see if they wanted to come, but there was no way. Marianna and Luke were doing their best Cirque du Soleil impersonation, wrapped around each other in a corner, and Lisa Marie was back in full regal mode, holding court in the middle of her circle of guys.

Okay, so she was outta there. Excellent.

Tony was wearing a white silk scarf draped around his neck when she spotted him in the lobby. He looked so calm and relaxed, Heather immediately felt the same way. It was so easy being around him. Was that a good sign? Did it mean she liked guys after all?

"Hey," he greeted her. "Just you? No friends?"

"They're doing their own thing," Heather explained.

Tony nodded. "It's better this way."

Uh-oh. How come? She tensed slightly at the thought of being alone with him, but he wasn't giving off any *I want to jump your bones* vibes, so she decided not to worry.

"So I'm parked in the garage. You want to just follow me?" he said.

Heather nodded, glad to be taking her own car. That way, she'd still be in control. She liked being in control. She could leave anytime she wanted, if the whole thing didn't suit her taste.

They drove up Connecticut Avenue and turned down some pretty, tree-lined side streets just across the line into Chevy Chase. Most of the houses were dark at this hour. Tony pulled up in front of a gray clapboard-covered house with a wide front porch and graceful columns. Lights glowed inside.

"Nick's parents are in Spain," Tony explained as they walked up the front steps.

He opened the front door without knocking and held it open for Heather. Inside, just past the entryway, she saw a large square living room where Nick's friends were hanging out. The place was decorated with exquisite Arts and Crafts furniture and a large, beautiful Oriental rug. Some people were curled up on leather chairs, others were sprawled on the rug, sipping champagne from crystal flutes or drinking from cut-crystal lowballs. They were watching a DVD on a large plasma screen high above the marble fireplace.

"Hey, everyone, this is Heather," Tony said, introducing her when someone paused the DVD.

There were about eleven people, girls and guys. Tony introduced her to Nick and tried to introduce a few others, but someone had unpaused the movie, and they'd gone back to watching it.

"Grab a drink," Nick said, gesturing toward the bar.

What a cool scene, Heather thought. So much hipper than the party she'd just left. Half as many people in three times as much space—that was a good start. And even though they were drinking, no one was being loud or disgusting. It was smokier than she liked, what with the cigarette smoke lingering in the air. But the ceilings were high, so the smoke rose up. It wasn't too hard to take.

I could get used to this, Heather thought. She instantly felt comfortable with this crowd. Most of them were film buffs—she recognized Talia and Jordan, who had both directed arty student films last year. The other guys were part of the hipster/film crowd at St. Claire's, the people who always wore black.

"What are we watching?" she whispered to Tony as he handed her a glass of champagne.

On the screen, a young Frank Sinatra was chewing up the scenery in some old black-and-white film. Corny, melodramatic music swelled in the background.

"Looks like *The Man with the Golden Arm,*" Tony answered.

"It is," the guy sitting on the floor near them said. "We're doing clips from our least favorite films. This one's my pick."

"Unbelievable music," Nick sneered as the orchestra

swelled to a dramatic crescendo. "Someone should've given the composer a Valium."

Everyone laughed.

"Yeah, well it *is* a film about drug addiction," the floor guy said.

"Okay, Valium for the composer, but the lighting guy could have used an upper," Talia joked. "I mean, what's with how dark this thing is?"

"There's a reason it's not called *film blanc*, Talia," someone said. "What do you expect?"

"I expect to be able to tell the difference between the actors and a carpet stain."

"Did you see that camera shadow?" Jordan called out. "You could see it in the whole opening shot."

"Wait . . . wait . . . here comes the worst part." The guy on the floor sat up and pointed at the screen. "Now watch. Frankie's going to leave the bar. Watch the jukebox . . . they're going to pull it out of the way . . . here it comes . . . to make room for the camera to get out the door."

Heather watched closely. This was fun. Yup—he was right. The jukebox slid out of the way, seemingly all by itself.

"I know it's Sinatra," the guy on the floor said, "but it doesn't deserve to be on a classics list."

Heather curled up in the corner of a plush couch and took another sip of her champagne. Yum. The bubbles felt good. Half a glass, and she already felt slightly tipsy. But it was all good. She wasn't designated to drive anybody at this point. And besides, by the time she left here, she'd be sober again.

"Okay, who's next?" Nick said, stopping the DVD.

Jordan handed him a different video, and Nick popped it into a player nestled in a carved wooden wall cabinet.

The movie came on. Instantly everyone started hooting and booing. It was Jennifer Garner in *13 Going on 30*.

"Talk about a bomb. This turkey nearly ruined her career," someone said.

"What career?" Tony joked.

"Yeah—she was so desperate after this movie bombed, she started dating Ben Affleck."

Heather laughed. It was refreshing to be with people who actually thought dating Ben Affleck was a comedown!

"Check out this cheesy glitter effect when she transforms into thirty," Jordan said.

"What—you'd prefer she just twitch her nose?" Talia said.

"No, I'd prefer the vaporization effect they used in *War of the Worlds*—for the whole *film*," Jordan joked.

"I haven't seen anything this cheesy since Tinkerbell."

"Hold on. We do *not* mock Tinkerbell," the guy on the floor said.

"Which one? The druggy Julia Roberts version in *Hook*? We mock that one all the time," Nick said.

"I stand corrected," Floor-guy said and bowed.

"Whoa! Check out the dress," Talia gasped. "They had better costume design in *March of the Penguins*."

"Better dialogue, too," Tony added.

Everyone laughed.

Funny! Heather thought. She couldn't quite keep up with these people—well, she couldn't top them, anyway—but she was loving the whole scene.

Jordan grabbed the remote and ran the DVD up to the party scene, where Jennifer Garner did an impersonation of John Travolta dancing in *Saturday Night Fever*.

"They should take away her Screen Actors Guild card for that," Nick commented.

"Yeah, that's the worst dancing I've seen since Hugh Grant in *About a Boy*."

"No, this is worse," Jordan argued. "It goes on much longer."

For the next half hour, they all took turns sticking DVDs into the player and screening the worst scenes from their favorite trashy films.

Then someone pulled out a porn DVD and popped it in the machine, as if it were just another movie.

Porn? Heather wasn't quite ready for that. She stiffened—poor choice of words?—waiting to see how it was going to change the mood of the party.

But apparently most of Tony's friends had seen this kind of thing before, because nobody flinched. They just went right on doing what they'd been doing before: ripping the film-making techniques apart, laughing, jeering, pointing out all the flaws.

The film was called *Knockers*, and it was about a door-to-door bra salesman who came in to sell skimpy lingerie to two twenty-something roommates.

"Listen to the echo on the set!" someone complained.

"You're too kind, calling it a set. That's obviously someone's living room."

"You're too kind, calling it a living room," Jordan shot back.

"Five points if you can spot a scene where the boom mic *isn't* showing in the top of the frame," someone said.

Everyone was silent for a minute, trying to win that challenge.

On the screen, the two women were trying on the lingerie and making out with the sales guy, who had gotten naked while they were in the kitchen getting him a beverage.

Heather held really still, not wanting it to show that she was squirming inside. The whole thing made her really uncomfortable. Who wanted to look at some guy's dick? Ick.

On the other hand, the two young women were a turn-on. She felt her face getting warm.

"Couldn't they put some makeup on his ass?" Talia complained. "I mean, please. He's got zits up the . . ." Her voice trailed off.

"Ass?" Jordan supplied.

More laughs.

"No, but watch this tracking shot," the guy who had

brought the porn DVD said. "The camera actually hits a bump on the carpet, and they just left it in."

"Oh God, you're right. Hey, look at that. They've used that same footage three times," Nick said.

On the screen, the salesman was doing something obscene with a hot dog bun.

"Yeah, and first he has the bun in his left hand. Then it's in his right. It's a total mess in terms of continuity," Jordan said.

Heather was so nervous, she didn't know where to look. Tony was sitting beside her on the sofa, although not too close. She could feel his radar scanning her . . . like, if she moved funny, or breathed strangely, or crossed her legs at the wrong time, he'd pick up on it and . . .

And what? He'd know? Know that she was gay?

I'm not gay, she thought. *I've never done anything gay in my life.*

On the screen, two women were kissing.

Heather couldn't take it anymore. She set down her glass of champagne, too hard. It made a loud clunk. Then she jumped up off the couch and dashed out of the room.

Chapter 24

Now that Li'l D was gone, Lisa Marie didn't know quite what to do with herself. She gazed around the suite at the disgusting mess. Crushed beer cans, empty plastic cups, discarded liquor bottles, overflowing ashtrays, and the torn wrappers from every single snack food in the minibar were strewn around the room.

Someone had spilled Raisinets on one of the beige upholstered chairs. Someone had sat on them. The same someone? It was a particularly unfortunate stain.

Was there anything so depressing as a trashed hotel room? she thought. It reminded her of the worst time of night at junior high sleepover parties, when girls would start trying to cut someone's hair in her sleep, or say something so hurtful that the birthday girl wound up crying and storming off to her room.

When the place looked like this, you knew things were going to get ugly.

"Lisa Marie, you want a beer?" Bradley drunkenly offered her a can and threw an arm around her shoulder, letting his hand dangle too close to her breast.

"Yeah, thanks," she said, taking the can and slouching away from his arm at the same time.

That was pretty sweet of him, wasn't it? she thought. Even after she'd pretty much ignored him all evening, here he was, being nice and bringing her a beverage. So what if the can was already half-empty? And had lipstick stains. She gave him a droopy-eyed smile.

Wow, I must be tired, she thought. Now even Bradley's attention was cheering her up. Not a good sign.

The room was emptying out—almost like someone had put up a sign: "This party died. Let it rest in peace."

"Hey, pretty girl." Marianna had pried herself out of Luke's arms and came over for a chat. "You having fun?"

"Definitely," Lisa Marie said.

Was she?

Her mood was roller-coastering. Ten minutes ago, she'd been high on Li'l D's four words: *"You, me, next time."* The next moment, she just wanted to curl up on the couch and go to sleep. Now she was up again. Why? Just because Bradley had given her a beer?

"I'm a little trashed," she admitted.

"Me, too. Guess what? Luke just called me his girlfriend."

"Well, he'd better! I mean, you've been giving him girlfriend privileges," Lisa Marie said, nodding toward the corner where Marianna and Luke had been making out.

Marianna giggled. "We're going down to the Lincoln Bedroom," she said, quickly explaining about the Lincoln Town Car.

"You go, girl," Lisa Marie said happily.

That sounded like a kick—a private Town Car in the basement of the hotel. Very remote. Very private. She wished she and Li'l D had wound up there tonight.

But it could still happen, Lisa Marie thought. Someday. Maybe she'd go with him to a recording session, and the studio would send a Town Car to pick them up. After, they'd tell the driver to take a hike while they made out in the back. Li'l D would call her his bitch in that soft, sexy way he had that didn't sound disrespectful. More like tender. Like the way he had said it tonight: *"Best-dressed bitch at the ball."*

He made the word sound like a caress.

"You okay here?" Marianna asked.

Lisa Marie looked around. John and Ramone were still there. Plus Marco and Bradley, and a few other people she didn't know. She'd be fine. She still had four guys to take care of her. Now, if Bradley would just bring her another beer . . .

"I'm good. Have fun," Lisa Marie said, giving Marianna a hug.

When Marianna and Luke had gone, Lisa Marie flopped down on an unstained couch, kicked off her shoes, and put her feet up on the coffee table.

Now what?

"Name two ways to fart," one of the guys said.

"I give up. What are they?" Marco asked.

"No, it's not a joke. I'm serious. I think there should be two ways to let 'em fly, but I can't think of them."

He was clearly the drunkest guy in the room. His shirt was open, and he was slumped on the couch near one of the two other remaining girls, a redhead.

"Oh, grow up, Andrew," the redhead said, shaking her head. "If there's one thing I can't stand, it's immature bathroom talk. Can we talk about something else?"

"You mean let's talk about you," the guy slurred. "Would that make you happy?"

"You not spitting when you talk would make me happier," she said, wiping at her cheek.

Besides the redhead and Andrew, there were just two other people left who Lisa Marie didn't know: a guy and a girl. She was wearing a fun retro fifties-style prom dress with a huge skirt made of pink netting. The guy was sprawled on the floor with his head in the girl's lap.

"I need a back rub," he said, looking up into her eyes.

"So turn over," she said.

"Yes!" the guy cheered, quickly turning to put his face in her crotch.

"Woooo!" Ramone shouted, egging them on.

But the girl quickly pushed him off and scooted away. "You *know* that's not what I meant! God!"

This was boring, Lisa Marie thought, feeling fuzzier by the minute. How come she was left with these people, instead of being off somewhere with Li'l D? She tried to think back, to remember what had happened, but it was kind of blurry. There must have been a moment where she could have done something differently . . .

"Lisa Marie, come sit with me," John said, patting his lap.

She ignored him, too tired to get up. "Marco's closer. Let him sit on you," she said.

"Awww." John pretended to pout.

"Here's my question," Marco said, sitting up like he just got a good idea. "How come we spent the whole night playing cards with all these girls in the room, and not one hand of strip poker?"

"It's never too late," Bradley said.

"Ha," the girl nearest Lisa Marie said. "You guys are so stoned, you'd be naked before I could say royal flush."

"I thought you said no bathroom talk," the drunk guy joked.

Everyone laughed.

Lisa Marie reached over to a torn bag of Sun Chips and dug inside for some crumbs. There weren't many, but she licked her finger anyway. The salt tasted good.

Someone yawned, and the redhead stood up to stretch. "Andrew, I'm starving, and we promised Emily we'd drop in at her party. Let's get out of here. You coming, Becca?"

The girl on the floor said yeah, she was ready to leave. Pretty soon the four of them were picking up stray bow ties, gathering up evening bags and jackets, and heading for the door. Then the redhead turned back and came over to Lisa Marie.

"Are you okay here?" she asked. Halfheartedly she added, "You could come with us."

"I'm fine."

That was nice of her, Lisa Marie thought. But she was too tired to go anywhere right then. And besides—she barely knew those people.

"Okay. Ciao."

The redhead, Becca, and the two other guys dragged themselves out the door.

Lisa Marie looked around the room and sighed. She was tired, but it was prom night. You didn't give up early on your senior prom. And besides, Marianna and Luke were busy downstairs. No way was she going to barge in on their private party.

"So what now?" she said, looking around at the four remaining guys.

John, Ramone, Marco, and Bradley. Her posse. Just like at Starbucks.

John shot a leering glance at Ramone, and they both laughed.

What's so funny? she thought.

Then she caught a look in Marco's eyes. There was a vibe in the room . . . a bad vibe. Suddenly she realized: She was alone in a hotel room with four drunk guys.

"Now we play that game of strip poker I was talking about," Marco said in no uncertain terms.

Chapter 25

What am I doing? Heather wondered as she dashed into the spacious kitchen at Nick's house.

She was wandering through a complete stranger's house, uninvited. Not normally her style—but this wasn't a normal night. Not by a long shot. How often had she sat in someone's living room watching porn with people she hardly knew?

That would be never.

For a minute she just stood there amid the granite countertops and glass-fronted cabinets feeling lost, not sure where to go next. The kitchen was just past the dining room, which was just off the living room. Not far enough away.

She could hear voices drifting in from the party, but they weren't laughing.

Were they talking about her?

Probably not. She wasn't that important to anyone there. But she still had an overwhelming impulse to escape.

She took a back stairway leading down and found herself in an elegantly decorated basement game room. There was a pool table, a mahogany bar, a dartboard, and another big-screen TV. A long nubby beige sectional sofa spanned two walls, and huge pillows cluttered the floor.

None of it looked worn. More like brand-new and barely used.

How ironic, Heather thought. Nick's parents had probably set up and furnished this game room specifically for him and his friends to have parties. But as soon as his parents were gone, they preferred to party upstairs in the living room, like adults.

That's what made them so cool, she decided. It's what had made her happy to be part of that group at first.

The sectional looked inviting. Heather plopped down on it and grabbed a pillow to hold on to. Maybe she could just curl up there and hide. Maybe no one would come looking for her. Maybe she'd even be left alone long enough to sober up—her head was still buzzing from that glass of champagne—and figure out how she really felt about sex.

Then again, maybe not. She heard footsteps on the stairs.

"Hey," Tony said with a soft tilt of his head, finding her. "You okay?"

Heather shrugged, and Tony came over to sit beside her.

"I just needed a break," she said, but her voice sounded shaky, even to herself.

Tony put an arm around her shoulder to comfort her. "What's wrong? Was that last movie a little too much for you?"

Yeah, Heather thought. *Too much in a lot of ways. Too much detail . . . too much information . . . too much stimulation . . . and way too many genders to choose from.*

How was she supposed to explain to him that just seeing all that sex on-screen had made her even more confused than she was before? Everything in the movie made her uncomfortable. So how was she supposed to sort out how she really felt?

There was only one way to find out, she decided. See if she could make herself fall for a guy. Make herself feel something. For someone like Tony.

After all, she liked Tony. He was sweet. A gentleman. A good artist. A good friend. He had all the qualities she would be looking for, if she were looking for a guy.

She turned her face toward him and without saying anything, leaned up and kissed him as passionately as she could. Tongue and all.

"Euhmn . . ." Tony pushed her away as fast as he could and sort of scooted over. "Whoa. What's this all about? I thought you were gay."

Heather blinked, embarrassed and totally shocked.

What? He thought she was gay?

"What would make you think *that*?" she demanded defensively.

Tony shrugged. "Takes one to know one, I guess," he said with a sheepish grin.

Heather's mouth dropped open. What a complete idiot she'd been! *Of course*. It made perfect sense. No wonder he hadn't dated anyone since Jenny Burkowski last year.

Tony sort of settled back into the couch cushions and let out a sigh that Heather recognized immediately. It was the sigh she'd been wanting to sigh herself—of having finally told someone the truth.

"I finally admitted to myself that I'm gay last year," Tony explained. "Jenny and I had been going out a long time, and not doing much, if you catch my drift. I guess I was in denial."

"Yeah. I'm familiar with that territory," Heather admitted quietly.

"Anyway, a week before the prom, Jenny started talking about how we should do something 'special' on prom night, and I had a sinking feeling I knew what she had in mind. But I just kept ignoring her. So there we were in my car one night and she ripped off her sweater in front of me."

"Oh my God. What happened then?" Heather asked.

"I flinched," Tony said, laughing at himself, "and she got the picture. She dumped me that instant."

"Wow. Everyone knows *half* of that story," Heather muttered.

"Yeah. The boring half."

"So she figured out you were gay, but she never told anyone?"

Tony nodded. "I'll always love her for that."

Heather had to smile at the way he said it. *"Love her."* He wasn't kidding, either. She could tell Tony really did love Jenny Burkowski in a way. Just not *that* way.

"Anyway, I'm still in the closet—obviously," Tony went on. "But I hate it."

"You've never told *anyone* else?" Heather's jaw dropped again. She couldn't believe she was the first.

"No, I finally told Nick a few months ago, and it felt great," he said. "But I haven't worked up the nerve to really come out. It sucks. I'm strongly recommending you not follow my example."

Heather smiled. It was so sweet of him to care about her this way—and he really did seem to care. She could tell.

"Honestly, you've got to set an example for me," he said with a teasing smile.

"What do you mean?"

"Just don't make yourself miserable the way I have. Come out to your friends, Heather—or at the very *least*, come out to yourself."

That last part made her smile so much, it almost hurt. She wanted to lean over and kiss him again—on the cheek, this time—but she wasn't sure he'd understand.

"I will if you will," she said, teasing him back.

He shook his head. "No promises here."

"Okay," she said slowly, realizing she couldn't push him and didn't want to. "That's fair. But maybe I will anyway. On my own."

Chapter 26

"It's hard to believe Lincoln actually slept here," Marianna joked, gazing around at the black leather seats in the Lincoln Town Car.

"Yeah, considering how tall he was," Luke said. "But I have it on good authority."

"Hah. What kind of proof have you got?" Marianna challenged.

"Just look at the trunk. It's got his name right on it."

Marianna laughed. She loved arguing with Luke—it was their favorite form of flirting. They were both so competitive, they felt most at ease when they were trying to win.

Luke eyed the length of the big, cushy backseat.

"On the other hand, you might be right," he said. "This thing's pretty short—for tall people."

"You trying to say you wouldn't fit on this bench seat?" Marianna teased, picking up on Luke's vibe. That's what he was getting at, wasn't it? That there wasn't much room for them to lie down?

"You probably wouldn't fit here, either," Luke said. "You're not a shrimp, Kazanjian."

He pulled her close to him and kissed her. Then he leaned forward a little more, still kissing her, and pushed her over gently. She slipped sideways and fell onto her back.

It was an awkward angle, and her feet hung off the end, but she didn't care. *My night in the Lincoln Bedroom,* Marianna thought, her head swirling with all kinds of emotions and feelings.

Actually, it wasn't just her head swirling. Half of the feelings were above the waist. Half below.

For a minute, Luke just lay on top of her, looking into her eyes. "You're beautiful, you know that?" he said.

"Umm." She *felt* beautiful right that minute, and she didn't want to lie.

Marianna beamed at him. How lucky could she get? Here she was, on prom night, with *the* guy—the one she'd been crushing on for months and months. And he really seemed to be into her.

He also seemed to be waiting for something. A signal? Like she was supposed to let him know how far to go?

Marianna held still, not sure how this part of the game

was played. She'd barely ever been kissed before Luke, let alone let some guy round the bases.

"I'm crushing your flower again," Luke said, looking down at her dress with a smile.

Marianna shrugged. "I told you—crush away."

"How about if I take it off?"

A sexy shiver ran through her body at the thought of him touching her dress up there. They'd been making out all night, but mostly just heavy kissing. He hadn't gone that far yet.

"Take off my corsage?" she said.

Luke nodded.

"Yeah. Okay."

He couldn't really manage it, given the positions they were in. Not until Marianna sat up. Then Luke gently unpinned her corsage from the strap of her gown. In the process, his fingers brushed her breast. He tossed the flower on the floor and kissed her again, passionately.

Before she knew it, they were making out heavily, and after a while—was it twenty minutes? longer?—she was on her back again, with her dress unzipped.

Oh, God, Marianna thought. Should she be doing this? She didn't really care about "should" anymore. All she knew was that she was wrapped up in the moment and didn't want to stop.

Luke put his hands under her dress, and she let out a moan. He looked deep into her eyes. "Is this okay?" he asked.

"Yes," she breathed into his ear, closing her eyes again and getting lost in the moment.

When the moment was over, Marianna opened her eyes and suddenly realized what had happened. Oh my God. She had just done it. The big It. She'd lost her virginity to Luke.

Luke lay beside her, sweaty and exhausted, breathing hard, not really seeing the expression on her face.

Wow, she thought, stunned. She hadn't been planning to go *that* far. Not this soon. She cared about Luke . . . a lot.

But they'd only been going out for a few weeks. What was this—their fourth date? Losing your virginity was supposed to be one of the greatest moments in a girl's life, not an accident.

Luke lifted his head and gazed at her.

"You okay?" he asked.

Marianna didn't know how to answer.

He leaned over her and kissed her nose. Then he caught a fragile expression in her eyes. "Hey . . . was that . . . ?"

"My first time." She nodded.

"I didn't know," he said, stroking her hair. "Are you sure you're okay?"

No, Marianna thought. *Not entirely.*

She wasn't sure how she felt, to tell the truth. Right that minute, all she could think was: her father would kill her if he found out.

And even if he didn't find out, she still felt guilty. Like

maybe she'd let *herself* down, never mind what her father thought.

She flashed on Coach Robinson's list of "Power Words for Winners." So much for *self-restraint.*

"What time is it?" she asked Luke.

He stretched forward to look at the clock on the dashboard. "Almost two."

"Oh, God." She'd meant to call her dad and give him the story about how she was staying at Lisa Marie's, but somehow that hadn't happened. "He probably has the police out looking for me," she muttered.

Luke looked slightly freaked out. "Really?"

"Well, yeahhhh."

Marianna wondered why he hadn't called yet. She was supposed to be home an hour and a half ago. It wasn't like her dad—or her mom, for that matter—to just let her be late and then deal with it later. Her dad was more the deal-with-it-right-this-damned-minute type.

Maybe her cell phone was dead?

She sat up, looking for her little evening bag. Before she could find it, her cell phone started to ring.

Uh-oh. Now what? If she answered it, her dad would scream at her and make her feel like a slut—and she absolutely couldn't take that right now.

Not tonight, of all nights.

But if she didn't answer, he would probably jump into his

car, come barreling down to the hotel, and make a scene. No joke. He'd done that kind of thing before.

"Are you going to answer that?" Luke asked.

"I have to find it first," Marianna said, digging through the pile of clothes on the limo floor.

Chapter 27

"Pick up your cards," Marco ordered Lisa Marie, tossing them at her one by one. "Like I said, it's time for a little strip poker."

"Not funny," Lisa Marie said. She moved away from the game table, but he flipped another card at her and it hit her in the chest.

"Not supposed to be funny," Marco said. "I think you owe us, don't you?"

"Yeah," Ramone agreed. "You played us, didn't you, Lisa Marie? Promising to hang with us, each one of us, and then no one winds up with anything. That's what I call a cock tease."

"Hey, don't say stuff like that." Bradley stepped forward. "She doesn't owe anybody anything."

"Thank you!" Lisa Marie felt vindicated.

"Except maybe an apology," Bradley said, his face turning sour.

Lisa Marie took a deep breath, trying to stay calm. Her heart was pounding hard, and she wanted to run. But her instincts told her: never show fear. If they saw she was afraid, it could get seriously dangerous.

"I don't know what you're talking about," she snapped, trying to sound as hard-ass as she could. A good offense was the best defense, right? Angela always said that. "I didn't play anyone. I just wanted to have fun tonight. If you guys got the wrong idea, that's your problem."

"No, it's your problem," Marco said harshly. There was such a mean edge in his voice, she felt like she'd been slapped.

With a leering smile on his face, he sauntered over to her. Lisa Marie had already edged away; she was backed against a wall now. He leaned both hands against the wall, surrounding her with his arms so she was trapped. "However," he said in a sickeningly syrupy voice, "I'd be happy to protect you from these goons . . . if you make it worth my while."

"Look at her squirm!" Ramone said, laughing. "She looks like a cornered little rat."

"How would you know what rats look like when they're cornered, Ramone?" Lisa Marie spat the words. "Oh, I forgot. You probably see them all the time at home."

Ramone's face turned hot red. Yeah—that was the right

button to push. One Hispanic to another, she knew what the buzzwords were that would make his blood boil.

Of course there was no way Ramone had rats anywhere near his suburban, middle-class house. He was a private school brat, just like she was. But if he was going to play rough, she could slap back, too.

Ramone threw a beer can across the room, sort of in her direction. It hit the lampshade, knocking it sideways.

"Keep it cool," Marco said to Ramone. "Everyone knows you drive a Lexus and live miles from the ghetto."

"Unlike Teeny Tiny D, who she's got the hots for," Ramone said jealously.

So that was it. Ramone was jealous of Li'l D. Maybe the others were, too? Well, who wouldn't be?

"Hey, I have an idea," John said. "Let's let her choose."

"Choose what?" She said it with as much hostility and edge as she could muster.

"Choose which one of us you want to be with," John said. He eyed her up and down, drinking in each curve and bump in her slinky satin number. "I mean, a body like that wasn't made to be wasted."

"Take a cold shower," Lisa Marie said to John, and then directed the rest of her comments to all of them. "Maybe you'd *all* like that. All four of you bunched up together in the shower? That must be what rocks your boat."

Marco shook his head and laughed. "You'll have to do better than that," he said. "Homophobe-bating? With St. Claire's guys? You must be kidding. We're an enlightened, tolerant, love-thy-neighbor bunch if ever you saw one."

"Oh, right. I just love all the enlightened things that have come out of your mouth tonight," she snapped at Marco.

"How about a few enlightened things going into yours?" John joked.

"Okay, that's it." Lisa Marie started to search the room for her bag. "I'm out of here."

Marco blocked her way. "No you're not."

Her heart raced even faster. Was he serious? Was this going to get as ugly as it felt?

She tried not to look scared and simply pivoted around to go another direction. But this time John put himself in her path.

"I say we play a game of poker to see who gets to go first with her," he said.

Ramone laughed hard. Too hard.

Every fiber of her being told her to get out now.

"I'm calling a cab," Lisa Marie said.

"No way." Marco dashed to snatch away the cordless phone from the hotel desk.

He held it high over her head, then tossed it to John, who laughed and flipped it to Ramone. For an instant, Lisa Marie did what she'd always done in grade school at times like this: turned one way, then the other, trying to grab the object away, always a moment too late.

Monkey in the middle.

"Woo-hoo! Look at her jump!" John mocked.

She stared at John, who was looking at her like he didn't intend this game to stop.

Panicked and fighting against the fear, she held very still and looked hard around the room for her bag. If she could get to her cell phone . . .

It was under the coffee table. She lunged for it quickly, but John was faster. He grabbed her around the waist. One hand went higher, groping her chest.

"Whoa," Bradley said. "That's not okay."

"Oh, shut up, Bradley," John snapped. "We're not hurting her."

"Get some balls, Bradley," Ramone sneered.

"Get your hands off me!" Lisa Marie screamed. She spun and twisted, trying to get away from John, but now Ramone was pulling her toward him, too.

"Hey!" Bradley's voice was loud and sharp and forceful. Everyone froze at the sound of it. "Leave her alone!"

"Yeah, right," John laughed.

Bradley lunged at John and shoved his shoulder hard, pushing him aside. "I mean it!" Bradley shouted. "Let her go or I'll call 911!"

Ramone stopped trying to grope her, and John let go, too. They both stood still, but they were scowling furiously.

"Okay, man," John spat the words at Bradley with hot anger. "But get her out of here."

Lisa Marie was shaking inside. Trembling, she bent down

to pick up her little evening bag, extremely aware that her dress was very low cut in back, and they were still all watching her ass. Right that minute, she didn't feel like the best-dressed girl at the ball. Not by a long shot.

When she stood up, Bradley walked over and put a comforting hand on her arm. "Come on," he said. "Let's get some fresh air."

Thank God, Lisa Marie thought. She wanted to hug him for being there and helping her out of this mess, but she definitely didn't want to give him any wrong signals. They'd had enough misunderstandings for one night.

Her legs were still trembling and shaky, partly from the adrenaline rush and partly because she was dizzy and still more or less trashed. She took Bradley's arm for support, and they silently marched out of the suite.

Her mind was fuzzy on the way to the elevator. What had just happened? How did it get so out of control? Were they really going to . . . to . . . attack her? Or were they just playing a sick, ugly game to scare her shitless—which, by the way, had worked.

Bradley pushed the down button. "You want to go hang in the lobby?"

Lisa Marie shook her head. Not the lobby. It was so public, and she was on the verge of tears. She definitely didn't want to be seen there looking wasted and falling apart on Bradley's shoulder.

"Just take me home," she said in a weak voice.

"I can't," Bradley said. "I didn't drive. I came with some other guys."

Shit. Now what? She tried to think, but her head was still spinning. She just didn't want to be seen looking like this. Like she imagined she looked.

"Can we just go somewhere private?" she asked. Then maybe she could call Heather or something, and figure out how to get home.

"Yeah."

When the doors opened on the lobby, a bunch of St. Claire's kids pushed into the elevator, staring as Lisa Marie got out.

I must look a wreck, she thought, quickly turning away from them toward a deserted hallway that led to some empty, unoccupied ballrooms. All she wanted right now was to hide somewhere, cover her face, and cry. Or sleep.

But definitely hide.

"Let's go in here," she said, leaning against the ballroom door and pushing it open with her backside.

It was a ballroom as big as the one the prom had been held in, but it felt totally different. No decorations, no mood lighting, no dance floor or disco ball. Just a few stacks of metal hotel banquet chairs off in one corner, and a baby grand piano in the other, covered with a canvas tarp. A few dim lights on the perimeter walls gave the room an eerie, abandoned feel.

At least it was quiet. And private. No one was going to come barging in on them here.

Bradley hadn't said much since they left the room, and Lisa Marie was glad. She didn't know what to say. She was too embarrassed about everything that had happened, and furious at the same time. Plus she felt too shaky to make small talk.

"You want to sit down?" he said, nodding toward the stacks of chairs.

Lisa Marie nodded.

Bradley hoisted two chairs off the stacks and set them side by side, in the darkest corner.

That was nice, Lisa Marie thought. He was really taking care of her. The dark felt soothing, protective. She dropped her bag on the floor, sat down on one of the chairs, and put her face in her hands.

"Hey," Bradley said, sitting beside her and putting a gentle arm around her shoulder. "Don't cry. Those guys are jerks."

"I'm not crying," she said, looking up. "I'm just . . . wrecked."

He pulled her closer.

"It's okay," he said, leaning in to give her a kiss.

Lisa Marie pulled back. "Hey." He was being sweet, but she was definitely not in the mood.

"What?" Bradley snapped. His arm was still around her, and she felt his hand tighten.

"Sorry . . . I just . . . I don't feel like . . ."

"Christ!" Bradley said. "You're the one who wanted to go somewhere private!"

Oh God, Lisa Marie thought. *Had he misunderstood? Again?* Instantly, she felt guilty. This had to be her fault, if guys kept getting the wrong idea. Didn't it?

She tried to clear it up quickly. "Sorry," she repeated. "I just wanted to come in here to get away from the crowds. I didn't mean . . ."

"I thought you'd be grateful," Bradley said angrily.

She stared at him, outraged. Was he kidding? He thought she *owed* him?

"Ramone was right," Bradley said. "You're a cock tease."

He grabbed her with both hands and leaned close, pressing his tongue into her mouth.

Stop it! Lisa Marie wanted to shout, trying to pull away from him.

But he was strong. And forceful. He groped her chest, then threw one leg over top of hers, making it very clear he didn't intend to stop there.

Chapter 28

Marianna dove for her evening bag, which was buried under a pile of shoes and various discarded items of Luke's clothing on the floor of the limo.

Wow, she thought. She hadn't even noticed that Luke took off his shirt.

The sound of her cell phone was faint, like it was some distant voice she'd forgotten all about. Where was the damned bag? Somehow, it had slipped under the front seat, under Luke's tux jacket. When she finally retrieved it and checked caller ID, she was astonished to see it wasn't her dad.

"That's weird. It's Todd." She gave Luke a puzzled glance as she flipped the phone open to answer. "Todd? What's up?"

"Hey, Marianna." His voice sounded nervous, tense. "Is Lisa Marie with you?"

Marianna rolled her eyes. It wasn't like Todd to turn into Stalker Boy, but emotions tended to run high on prom night. Maybe he'd been drinking too much . . .

"Listen, Todd, you've got to chill about her. You can't do this. Back off and let her have a life. You *dumped* her, remember?"

She was trying to be patient and understanding with the guy, but God—he had just interrupted the most important event of her life.

"No, no, that's not it," Todd struggled to explain. "I'm worried about her. I think she might be in trouble."

Marianna pursed her lips and took a minute to evaluate. Was it a ploy? He sounded pretty upset.

"What kind of trouble?"

"She was up in the suite with a bunch of guys," Todd said carefully, logically, like he didn't want to jump to any conclusions but he couldn't ignore a preponderance of the evidence. "I think she was one of the last girls there. Anyway, I just heard some guys in the elevator saying that John and Ramone were going to have a little fun with her."

"Oh, no."

"Yeah. It sounded ugly. They were saying John wanted to get back at her for playing them or something."

Marianna started putting on her shoes as fast as she could.

"Get dressed," she whispered to Luke, covering the phone. Then back into the phone she said, "Did you go up to the suite?"

"I can't remember what room it was." Todd sounded embarrassed. "That's why I called."

"Luke, what room was the party in?" Marianna asked.

"Huh?"

Now that her eyes were open and she was sitting up and adrenaline was racing through her body, Marianna noticed that Luke looked fairly blotto. His eyelids drooped, and he sort of swayed as he tried to put on his shirt.

"Lisa Marie's in trouble," Marianna said. "What room was the party in?"

"Um . . . 1567? Something like that."

That sounded right. Something like that. "Try 1567," she told Todd. "Or 1675. Hurry! We'll meet you up there."

Her mind was a blur, trying to function in the harsh present instead of the intimate haze she and Luke had just been lost in.

She closed her phone, noticing as she did that she had five "missed calls." So her dad had been calling after all. Probably while she was at the party, which was such crazy chaos. No wonder she didn't hear the phone ring.

He probably *did* have the police looking for her right now.

Luke was slow putting on and tying his shoes, trying to find the studs for his shirt, tucking the shirttails into his pants. He didn't want to go up to the hotel lobby in his bare chest, and she couldn't blame him for that, but this was an emergency.

God knows what they were doing to Lisa Marie . . .

Marianna needed help zipping up the back of her dress. It

was awkward, sitting sideways and half kneeling on the floor of the car so Luke could do it. She wished he'd hurry up. She wished he weren't so clumsy with it. She almost wished her mother was there to zip it instead.

Finally they tumbled out of the Lincoln Bedroom and stumbled through the parking garage to the elevator.

Luke pushed the button over and over. The elevator didn't come.

"Shit! Should we take the stairs?" She looked around for them, trying to figure out how many levels down they were from the lobby.

"What did Todd say?" Luke asked, bleary-eyed.

"He said Lisa Marie was in trouble!" Marianna snapped, taking her anxiety out on him.

Luke was so sweet, he didn't even show an ounce of anger. He just wrapped an arm around her shoulders and pulled her toward the stairs. "Come on," he said. "This is probably faster."

Just then, the elevator doors opened. They raced back and dashed in just before the doors closed again.

In the elevator, Marianna took out her cell phone to call Heather. Not that Heather could help—she was God knows where, at a party halfway across town. But when the chips were down, Heather had always been their rock. She was the one Marianna and Lisa Marie could count on.

Her hands shook as she dialed the number. "Come on, Heather. Pick up."

What could she be doing that was so important she wouldn't answer her phone?

It rang five times, then the voice mail clicked in.

"Heather, it's me. When you get this, call me," Marianna said, trying to keep her voice calm. "Lisa Marie's in a bad situation. We're still at the hotel, and Luke's here, and I'm sure everything's going to be all right and everything . . . but just in case, could you get your butt back here? Now?"

Chapter 29

"Did you go up to the suite? Is she okay?" Marianna demanded when she and Luke found Todd standing in the lobby.

"You gave me the wrong room number," Todd sounded frustrated and angry. "I woke some woman up, and she wasn't too happy about it."

"Oh, God. What room was it?" Marianna turned to Luke, pleading for him to remember. If something happened to Lisa Marie, it would be her fault for getting it wrong . . .

Her head hurt, and she knew she wasn't thinking too clearly. But she wasn't exactly drunk anymore either. There was something about losing your virginity—it sobered a girl up real quick.

"I'm not sure," Luke admitted, still sounding fuzzy. "Maybe 1567?"

"That's the room I already tried!" Todd almost shouted.

"Let's just find her." Marianna headed for the bank of elevators, hurried into one, and pushed the button for the seventeenth floor. A crowd of drunken conventioneers got into the elevator with them.

"I think it was 1756," Marianna said to Luke. "That sounds right, doesn't it?"

He shrugged. "I'm not sure."

The elevator was so slow. It stopped on five, eight, and nine, for people to get off. Then it stopped on twelve because some jerk had pressed the up button when he wanted to go down.

Finally they reached the seventeenth floor and dashed into the hall. Luke came to a halt and stared at the wall, trying to decode the signs.

Rooms 1712 through 1747 were to the right. Rooms 1748 through 1765 were to the left. Marianna felt dyslexic, trying to figure out which way to go.

"This way," Todd said, Mr. Level-Headed-in-a-Crisis. He hurried down the corridor to the right.

We're runners, Marianna thought. What the hell are we waiting for?

She took off her shoes and threw them aside as she dashed down the long hall, bumping into Todd on the way. Luke was right behind her. As usual.

When she found the room, she started ringing the doorbell, over and over.

"Come on!" She was trying not to shout because she

didn't want to wake people who were sleeping. But could someone please answer the frigging door?

Oops. So much for not waking anyone up.

A middle-aged man in navy pajamas and half-shut eyes opened the door a crack. "What the hell do you want?" he asked.

Marianna checked the door number again: 1756. That was the right number, wasn't it?

Maybe not.

"Sorry. I guess we have the wrong room," she apologized, then turned and hurried back to the elevator, picking up her shoes on the way.

"Wait!" Luke called, catching up. Suddenly he seemed sober. "I think I remember. It was on the sixteenth floor."

"Are you sure?"

"No. But I think so."

They pushed into the elevator, squeezing in with a family of four who were checking in at this ridiculous hour. They had four pieces of luggage, and the kids looked sleepy.

Todd stared at the buttons. "Yeah, I think Luke's right. The party was on sixteen. I'm pretty sure because someone pushed the button when we were coming up to the party, and it was in the left-hand row . . ."

No one cares what row it was, Marianna thought. *Just please, be right.*

Todd pushed sixteen, but the elevator lurched upward.

Oh, God, this car was going the wrong way. Of course.

These people were checking *in.* They obviously weren't heading *downstairs* with all that luggage. Shit. They'd gotten into the wrong elevator.

By the time they got to sixteen, Marianna was beginning to panic. What if they didn't find her in time? What if it was already too late? What if . . .

John and Ramone were animals. Everyone knew they couldn't keep their dicks in their pants.

Everyone except Lisa Marie.

They dashed out of the elevator, and Luke instinctively turned to the right, toward the room they'd been in earlier that night.

Yeah, this seemed right, Marianna thought. She remembered that flower painting on the wall, near the decorative hall table. It reminded her of a painting her aunt had in her bathroom.

"I think it's 1657," Luke said.

She and Luke hurried ahead and rang the bell. No answer. She pounded on the door and pushed the bell four or five more times.

Nothing. It was silent in there.

Across the hall, they could hear someone's television playing in another room.

"Do you really think this is the right room?" Marianna asked Luke.

"Yeah," he said. "I do."

"Then why is it so quiet in there?"

Luke, Todd, and Marianna all stared at each other for a moment. Todd looked really upset, but he was trying to hold it together.

"Maybe it's a good sign." Luke tried to be positive. "I mean, maybe they're gone. She can't be in much trouble if she's not in there."

But what if she's in there, and she can't call out for help? Marianna thought.

"I'll bet they went to another party," Todd started to say.

Just then, the door opened.

Marco stood there glaring at them in his boxers. "What?"

Marianna's throat tightened. Boxers? Oh, man.

"Where's Lisa Marie?" she demanded.

Luke didn't wait for an answer. He pushed his way into the room, and Marianna followed him. "Where is she?"

"Jesus! Get the hell out of here!" Marco shouted. "She's not here. She left."

No way was Marianna taking his word for it. Neither was Todd. They quickly searched the place, which didn't exactly take long.

The suite was empty, except for Marco, who had apparently been lying on the bed watching pay-per-view, which was still playing silently on the TV.

"So what happened?" Marianna demanded. "Where are John and Ramone? What did you guys do to Lisa Marie?"

"I told you," Marco said angrily. "She left about fifteen minutes ago. With Bradley."

"Just Bradley?" Marianna was skeptical.

Marco nodded. "John and Ramone split to some other party, but I'm too beat."

Marianna eyed him coldly, trying to decide whether he was telling the truth. He didn't seem to be lying. And anyway, Lisa Marie was obviously not there now.

"Okay. Sorry, man," Luke said. "We just heard she might be in trouble. We'll get out of your way."

What a mess, Marianna thought as they left the room. Trash everywhere. It didn't look like anyone could possibly have been having fun in there.

When they were back in the hall, she turned to Luke. "So do you think we should keep looking for her?"

"Nah," Luke said. "She might be having fun. I mean, do you think she'd want us barging in on her and Bradley? You know what I mean?"

"I guess not," Marianna agreed.

Todd shook his head. "I'm going to keep looking till I find her," he said. "Just in case."

Marianna followed Todd toward the elevator, not sure what to think about that. Was he really just trying to protect Lisa Marie? Or was he trying to spoil her night? It was hard to know. Maybe he was turning into Stalker Boy after all . . .

Their eyes met in the elevator, and he gave her one of those classic Todd looks that said, *Ask me anything, and I'll tell you the truth.*

Okay. She didn't have to ask. She knew him. He was one of the good guys.

"Let's go with him," she told Luke as they reached the lobby and the elevator opened.

A pack of St. Claire's prom-nighters were trying to get on the elevator just as Marianna, Luke, and Todd got off. Two of them were girls Marianna had known since kindergarten, when they'd all had a crush on Michael Zemiska, and had orchestrated a wedding in the dress-up corner, taking turns being his bride. Michael had refused to play, but that hadn't been too much of a problem. A large Barney doll had stood in for the groom.

Both of the girls were named Amanda. Neither of them could stand Marianna anymore, and she couldn't stand them. But who cared?

"Have you seen Lisa Marie?" she asked them.

Amanda J. shook her head.

Amanda B. shrugged. "I saw her with Bradley a few minutes ago. They were headed down that hallway." She pointed as if she couldn't care less.

Todd hurried forward, waiting for no one. Marianna and Luke had to move it to keep up with him. The hallway led to a bunch of empty ballrooms and meeting rooms, and not much else. What were the chances Lisa Marie and Bradley were down here?

Todd tried the first meeting room door they came to, but it was locked.

He hurried on to the next one. Marianna tried a ballroom door across the hall. It opened.

Inside, the lights were dim, but she heard some muffled sounds coming from a dark corner.

It took a minute for her eyes to adjust to the dark, but when they did, she heard a yell and recognized the unmistakable black satin of Lisa Marie's dress.

Someone was on top of her.

"Oh, my God!" she yelled, racing forward. "Oh, my God!"

Chapter 30

"Get off me, you pig!" Lisa Marie was screaming as Marianna ran toward the dark, writhing shapes in the corner.

"Luke!" Marianna yelled, in case he didn't know where she was.

Not necessary. Both Luke and Todd had followed her into the ballroom and were racing toward the corner, shouting and cursing at Bradley at the tops of their lungs.

At the sound of all the commotion, Bradley jumped off Lisa Marie, but not before Marianna got a look at what was happening. He was practically on top of her, one knee on the chair, pinning her down with his body.

"Bradley, you goddamn prick!" Lisa Marie screamed as Luke and Todd pulled him away from her. "You asshole! God! You're such a fucking prick!"

"What the hell were you doing to her!" Todd screamed, but Bradley jerked away from him and beat a path out the door.

Marianna raced over to Lisa Marie, who, thank God, was still dressed but shaking like a leaf, hunched over, hugging her chest with her arms. "Are you okay?" Marianna asked, kneeling down beside her.

Lisa Marie burst into tears and covered her face in her hands. Her sobs were terrible, convulsive sobs. Marianna hoped they were mostly the aftereffects of fear and relief that Bradley was gone. It seemed from the looks of things, and from the sound of Lisa Marie's crying, that she was physically okay. Bradley hadn't gotten very far.

She turned to Luke and Todd, who were frozen, not sure what to do or say.

Todd looked a little bit afraid to make a move, but he cautiously came forward and sat down beside Lisa Marie, on the other chair.

"Lisa Marie? Are you okay?" he asked tenderly.

She nodded, still crying.

He slipped an arm around her shoulder gently, like he knew she might not want to be touched, but she leaned into him and let him hold her for a minute. She looked like a small child, happy to be back in her parents' arms.

"What an asshole!" she said, still choked with tears.

"Totally," Todd said. "I'm going to kill him."

"No, you're not." Lisa Marie shook her head firmly and glared at him. Everyone knew Todd wasn't the type to kill anyone, and besides, she didn't want him to do anything stupid.

She sobbed again and hid her face in his shoulder, still hunched over like she was protecting herself. "I'm such an idiot."

"No way," Todd said firmly. "It wasn't your fault. He's an asshole. You know that, right?"

She shook her head inconclusively.

"Lisa Marie? You know it wasn't your fault—right?" Todd said.

"It *totally* wasn't your fault," Marianna chimed in. Stupid as it was, she felt if it was anyone's fault—other than Bradley's—it was hers, Marianna's. Of course that wasn't logical, any more than Lisa Marie blaming herself was logical. But that's how it felt.

Lisa Marie dried her face with her hands. No one seemed to have a tissue.

"Thanks," she said to Todd, as if the word was way too small for what she was trying to say. She looked grateful for all his moral support. Then she tried to smile up at Luke, and thanked him, too. "But if you don't mind, I just want to be alone now. With Marianna."

"Oh—yeah. Definitely," Todd said, jumping up. He was always superconsiderate. "But are you really okay? I mean, getting home and everything?"

"We'll call a cab or something," Marianna said. "Don't worry."

"Okay."

The two of them looked like they didn't want to just abandon the girls right then, but Marianna made a gesture so they'd go.

When they were gone, Marianna sat down beside Lisa Marie and waited, not sure whether to ask questions or just let her cry some more. She looked so fragile and scared, like she wasn't sure the ordeal was over yet.

"I don't want to go home in a cab," Lisa Marie said.

"Don't worry," a voice said, coming toward them. "You won't have to."

Chapter 31

Heather pulled out a pocket pack of tissues from her evening bag as she strode toward Lisa Marie and Marianna.

"Thank God you're here," Marianna said, happy to see the one person she trusted enough to totally drop her guard. Heather had always been their rock, and just having her there was a huge relief. Her face was pink, her large gray eyes were clear and bright, and her stockings didn't have any runs. She looked like she knew what to do next—like she could handle whatever needed handling.

"What happened?" Heather asked, giving Lisa Marie a tissue and then taking another chair off the stack so she could sit with them. She pushed the chair close to Lisa Marie, so Lisa Marie was flanked on each side by her two best friends.

Then she looked over Lisa Marie's head at Marianna. "I got your message. God, Marianna."

God, Marianna. It was a slight rebuke, but okay—probably deserved. Maybe she shouldn't have said that Lisa Marie could get permanently hurt. But hey—you never knew what could happen when things like this spiraled out of control.

"Bradley attacked her." Marianna explained it as simply as she could. It didn't seem like the time to press Lisa Marie for more details.

Lisa Marie shuddered, and suddenly Marianna was sorry she'd used the word *attacked*.

"Oh, sweetie." Heather's voice was so comforting. She gave Lisa Marie a hug.

"They *all* did. They're all assholes," Lisa Marie spat out the explanation they'd been waiting for.

Heather gulped and shot Marianna a questioning glance. *How bad was it?*

Marianna shrugged. She didn't know.

"Oh, God." Heather hugged her again.

Just having her two friends there seemed to give Lisa Marie strength. She dried her eyes, for the first time looking like she wasn't going to cry anymore. Marianna wasn't sure what to do next, but Heather took charge. She got them on their feet and down to the parking garage and into the car. Perfect designated driver form.

Marianna gasped when she saw the clock in Heather's car. It was almost three A.M.

"I should call my dad," she mumbled from the backseat.

"Maybe you should call him from Lisa Marie's," Heather said. "Tell him we dropped her off first—and that's why you're going to be late?"

"No, you guys have to spend the night," Lisa Marie said. "Please? I don't want to be alone."

"Whatever you need," Heather said reassuringly.

Actually, that's perfect, Marianna thought. No way did she want to go home and face her father. She flipped her cell phone open and checked the call log. Yeah—now she'd missed *seven* of his calls. He'd probably left a bunch of furious, threatening, manipulative messages, like "You'll be going to air-conditioning school if you don't get your butt home instantly."

She could listen to them later. Or never.

The lights were still on in the kitchen when Heather pulled into Lisa Marie's driveway. Lisa Marie's mother came to the back door and peered out when she heard the car.

"I can't take it," Lisa Marie said wearily, making no move to get out of the car. "I don't want to tell them what happened."

"Come on," Heather said, getting out. "I'll tell them. It'll be okay."

Marianna had to wind her way through stacked-up bags

of potting soil, assorted clay pots, and dozens of little plastic containers of pansies on the Santoses' back deck to get into the house. Lisa Marie and Heather were right behind her.

Mrs. Santos held the door open and gazed into each girl's eyes as they walked in.

"I've been so worried," Mrs. Santos said to Marianna, who came through the door first. "Is everyone all right?"

Before Marianna could answer, Mrs. Santos caught sight of her daughter. In the bright light of the kitchen, Marianna saw for the first time that Lisa Marie's eye makeup was streaked down her face.

"Ay, hija, querida, estás bien? Qué pasa?" She rushed to hold her daughter in her arms. "Are you okay?"

"I'm okay, don't worry," Lisa Marie said, letting her mother hug her. *"No te preocupes."*

Mrs. Santos looked from Heather to Marianna, her face worried. Marianna wasn't sure what to say.

"It was a bad night, but she's fine, Mrs. Santos. Really," Heather explained.

There was a moment of strained silence, but Mrs. Santos finally nodded. "You must be tired after such a long night. And hungry? Do you want something to eat?"

Wow. Marianna wanted to kiss this woman for not prying or demanding all the gory details. It was obvious something bad had happened to her daughter, but here she was, letting Lisa Marie handle it herself, in her own way.

"I'd love a piece of raisin toast," Lisa Marie said, her voice still small like a tired child.

"With cinnamon?" Her mother gave her a knowing smile.

Lisa Marie's mouth turned slightly upward for the first time in hours. "That would be great, *Mama*. And can Marianna and Heather sleep over?"

"Of course," Mrs. Santos said. "I've already talked to Marianna's father three or four times, by the way. I'll call him again, now that you're here."

Marianna's eyes opened wide, shocked. "You've talked to my dad? And he didn't go all ballistic?"

"He was a little upset," Mrs. Santos said, obviously understating the case, "but Herman and I managed to convince him that if anything was really wrong, you girls would have called us."

Yeah, Marianna thought. That was probably true. They would have called the Santoses—eventually. Lisa Marie's parents never acted like the world was coming to an end if you did something wrong.

Lisa Marie led the way to her bedroom upstairs. It was a girly room, all ruffles and lace, still decorated the way she'd wanted it when she first moved to the U.S. Marianna liked it, even though it had a major Barbie aesthetic going on. The flounces and white eyelet canopy bed all seemed homey and safe and comforting—like Lisa Marie's parents.

Lisa Marie flopped down on the bed in her gown. It was wrinkled by now, and streaks of beer stains dotted the front.

"So do you want to tell us what happened?" Heather asked, perching on a desk chair.

Lisa Marie shook her head, her hair rubbing the pillow. "I'll tell you in the morning," she promised. "I'm so exhausted. I just want to sleep."

"Okay," Heather said. "But don't sleep in your dress—it'll make you feel like Euro-trash in the morning."

For half an instant, the word *trash* made Marianna flinch. Would Lisa Marie take offense or think Heather meant something by it? But then she realized how great it was that Heather would go ahead and say it—just say whatever she would have said yesterday—rather than tiptoeing around just because of what had happened.

Heather went to Lisa Marie's closet and rummaged for a nightgown. Eventually she came out holding three—one for each of them. They took turns using the hall bath to get changed, and while Marianna was in there squeezing into a pink flowered nightgown that was six inches too short, Mrs. Santos brought up some extra blankets, sleeping bags, and pillows. Plus cinnamon raisin toast for all.

"I talked to your father," Mrs. Santos called through the bathroom door. "He's fine with you spending the night."

"Thank you," Marianna called back.

It was like junior high. Marianna slept on the floor right next to Lisa Marie's bed, and Heather made a comfy place for herself on the floor near the window seat.

Before she knew it, Marianna was drifting off, half

dreaming and half reliving her private time with Luke in the Lincoln Bedroom, over and over in her sleep.

Sun streamed in through the shutters, drawing wide bands of light and dark on Marianna's face, and forcing her to wake up whether she was ready or not.

She opened one eye and closed it again immediately. Ugh. Her head still hurt, her eyes felt puffy, and without even looking, she knew they were the size of marshmallows. But not the same color.

"It's about time," Heather said, startling Marianna into opening both eyes and squinting up from the bedroom floor. "We're hungry! We've been awake for hours. Come on—get dressed!"

Marianna gazed at Heather, who was sitting there looking fresh as the morning dew in a pair of jeans and a cute, albeit outdated, little blue cotton sweater. Lisa Marie, on the other hand, was nowhere to be seen.

"Where did you get clothes?" Marianna asked. Lisa Marie was so much shorter than they were, those couldn't possibly be her jeans.

"Angela left some stuff in her closet." Heather nodded down the hall. "Help yourself. We're going out for breakfast."

Once she was vertical, Marianna's head cleared. She dressed quickly, wishing she'd gotten to the outdated little blue sweater first, because all that was left now were heavy winter sweaters and an oversized Duke University sweatshirt, left over from some old high school boyfriend of Angela's.

Oh, well. At the least the sweatshirt was blue—she looked great in blue.

Outside, she took a deep breath of cool, clear, morning air as they climbed into Heather's Saturn.

"You're both so great," Lisa Marie said the minute they were out of her house. No one had been talking much until then, not wanting to be overheard by Mr. and Mrs. Santos. They were clearly dying to know what had happened last night but had still somehow managed to restrain themselves from prying. "What am I going to do next year without you two?"

"Unlimited nights and weekends," Heather said, and all three of them laughed.

"So . . . do you feel like talking?" Marianna broached the subject first.

Lisa Marie nodded. "Definitely. But you go first. How was it in the Lincoln Bedroom?"

How *was* the Lincoln Bedroom? Marianna thought. She'd been thinking about that and dreaming about it all night. Luke had been amazing . . . the prom had been amazing . . . and she couldn't wait to order breakfast this morning, because blueberry pancakes were now her favorite food in the whole wide world. She'd never be able to eat them again without remembering how it felt to be in those hotel corridors and that hotel kitchen with him.

She told Heather and Lisa Marie everything that had happened. All the good, and all the rest. About how she had gotten so carried away in the heat of the moment that she'd whispered "Yes," and before she knew it, they'd gone all the way.

"Wow." Lisa Marie was almost speechless. "That's even bigger than my night."

Heather had a faraway look on her face—which, by the way, happened a lot lately, now that Marianna thought about it. But she quickly snapped into focus. "So are you glad? I mean, was it what you wanted?" Heather asked.

That was the million dollar question, wasn't it? Marianna had been asking herself the same thing all night.

"Honestly? I'm not sure. I mean, I really like him. I just . . . you know . . ."

"Didn't plan to do it?" Lisa Marie finished her sentence.

"Yeah. Not last night, anyway. I don't know—I guess we were both a little drunk. I'm not sure it would have happened otherwise. And yeah, it feels weird to have done it without planning it and deciding in advance and everything. I guess I'll have to think about it for a while to know whether it was a good thing or a mistake."

"Did you at least use protection?" Lisa Marie asked, not criticizing, just hoping for the best.

Marianna nodded. "Luke was prepared. And by the way, if he hadn't been, I *never* would have let it happen. It's not like I wasn't in control or didn't know what I was doing."

That was the important part, she suddenly realized. Whether she liked her own choices or not, at least she'd made them herself. She was responsible for what happened to her—she, alone. Not Luke. And certainly not her father.

"You know, the one thing I'm glad about is that I don't think I'm afraid of my dad anymore," she told them.

"Really?" Lisa Marie said. There was a pause. "*I'm* still afraid of him."

Funny, Marianna thought. But then, Lisa Marie hadn't taken charge of her life and made big decisions for herself, the way Marianna had. Oh, sure—some of the big decisions were made under the haze of a lot of alcohol and passionate romance, but so what? She knew what she was doing. Drunk or sober, she was still herself. It was her body and her life. Now that she'd taken the big step that was supposed to make her into a woman, she wasn't going to act like daddy's little girl anymore.

"So does this mean I don't have to go on your dates with you and Luke anymore?" Heather joked.

"Yeah," Marianna said, nodding slowly. She hadn't thought of that, but why not? She should tell her dad the truth about dating Luke. No more sneaking around like a child. "Yeah—I'll come out to my dad about it. That's a brilliant idea."

Heather gave the strangest little laugh.

The waitress came to take their order, and Marianna felt giddy. "Blueberry pancakes," she said, grinning ear to ear. "And bacon. No syrup."

"Okay, Lisa Marie. Your turn," Heather said when the waitress had gone. "What did those assholes do to you?"

Lisa Marie gave a deep sigh and swirled her coffee. Little by little, she told them what had happened in the suite when she was alone with the four guys. How John, Marco, and Ramone had gotten way out of line, groping her, taunting her, refusing to let her leave.

"The worst part was how they treated me like I deserved it," Lisa Marie said.

"Outrageous!" Heather shook her head. "They're such assholes."

"I know," Lisa Marie said. "I know it's not my fault, but it still feels like it is."

"Oh, no, you don't," Marianna said. "There's no way what happened is your fault."

Lisa Marie shrugged. "I know. But I just . . . I wish I hadn't made so many dates. That part was a mistake."

Yeah, it probably was, Marianna thought. But she wasn't going to say so. Lisa Marie was beating herself up too much already.

"So what happened with Bradley?" Heather asked.

"Jesus, what a joke," Lisa Marie said. "He acted like he was going to protect me from those jerks, and then he was ten times worse! If you hadn't gotten there . . ."

Her voiced trailed off.

"You'd be at the police station, pressing charges right now?" Heather said.

Lisa Marie nodded.

That was a sobering thought. Marianna couldn't even imagine how scary it must have been.

"Thank God Todd called us," she said. "And thank God I answered my phone. And thank God one of the two Amandas knew where you went . . ."

Really, they'd all been lucky.

"Todd was pretty great," Lisa Marie admitted.

"He was fantastic," Marianna agreed. "I thought he was just being a stalker, but no. He was watching out for you."

"He must be an incredible guy," Heather said. "I mean, even though you wouldn't take him back, he still seems to care about you."

"Yeah . . . I know." She took a big bite of her Belgian waffle slathered in strawberry topping. "You think I should get back with him, don't you?"

"Maybe," Heather said. "He seems like first-class boyfriend material to me."

Lisa Marie shook her head. "He's still boring," she said. "I'm looking for someone more . . ."

"More like Li'l D?"

"Yeah. Something between boring and asshole would be good."

"So do you think you have a chance with Drew?" Marianna asked. "I saw you two talking at the party. He looked pretty into you."

"Did he?" Lisa Marie's face lit up. Then she shook her

head firmly. "No—I mean, I really like him, and maybe we'll hook up sometime. But I'm thinking I need some space right now. Without guys, you know?"

Marianna felt sad. "No, you can't do that. Don't let this whole thing make you scared or turn you into a victim."

"No, that's not it at all," Lisa Marie explained. "I just want to feel good about myself—without worrying what other people think. You know?"

"That sounds like a plan," Marianna nodded.

Funny, she thought. She and Lisa Marie had just gone through totally different things . . . but they were coming out of it with the same agenda.

"Bottom line, I know I got myself into that situation," Lisa Marie said.

Marianna and Heather both opened their mouths to serve up the standard reassurances: It wasn't her fault, the guys were jerks and were totally responsible for their actions, blah blah blah. But Lisa Marie shut them up.

"And I *know* it wasn't my fault, yadda yadda yadda. You don't have to keep telling me that. But I don't want to be giving anybody mixed messages from now on, either." Lisa Marie declared it like she'd made up her mind, and she was proud of it.

So who was going to argue with that?

They called the waitress over for coffee refills. After she left, Marianna thought it was time to face the music and apologize to Heather.

"So how was your night?" she said, turning to Heather. "And before you tell us how much it sucked, just let me say I am sooooo sorry we dumped you all night long."

"Oh, me, too," Lisa Marie said, instantly and sincerely apologetic. "We were horrible. I just got so wrapped up with all those guys, I totally lost track of time, and it must have seemed like we blew off being with you all night."

Heather smiled like she had an amazing secret.

"What?" Marianna asked, catching the twinkle in Heather's eyes. "Did something happen with Tony? Was it juicy? Oh my God, are you in love?! Tell us!"

Heather practically spat her coffee, she was laughing so hard at the questions. "Well, actually, it was the best night of my life," she declared, beaming. "And to answer your questions, yes, yes, and yes. But it's not what you think."

Lisa Marie squealed with delight, like she was thrilled to be back on ordinary lightweight love-life problems. "Tell us everything."

Heather took a deep breath. "Okay, I'm going to cut to the chase here, because otherwise, I'm afraid I won't say it." She took another deep breath. More like she was hyperventilating. "I finally came to accept a truth about myself last night. I'm gay."

Marianna's mouth dropped open. What a shocker! It took a moment to process it, but then all at once it made perfect sense.

So *that* was it. No wonder! Like the gears in a slot

machine, her brain clicked through all the stuff that had been so hard to explain about Heather. That she wasn't into guys. That she didn't want to be manipulated into a hookup with Tony. That she froze every time Marianna talked about Luke's tongue down her throat. It all made sense.

"Wow," Lisa Marie said. "That's . . . amazing! And it's so . . . cool! I mean, you telling us. I feel totally honored."

"Me, too," Marianna chimed in quickly. "God . . ." She ran through all the inappropriate things she'd said to Heather, considering. "I feel like an idiot for not knowing."

"*You?* How do you think *I* feel?" Heather laughed, though it wasn't really a joke.

Marianna laughed. "Yeah. I guess." Her head was racing with questions. "But how long have you known? I mean, you didn't just realize it last night, did you?"

Heather shrugged. "I guess I've known for a while. But I was having a hard time with it."

Lisa Marie nodded. "I'll bet it was awful trying to hide it."

"Painful," Heather admitted.

"Wow," Marianna said, still amazed at this news.

"So wait, does that mean something happened with a girl last night?" Lisa Marie's eyes lit up. "Tell us everything!"

Heather hesitated, but a smile crept across her lips. "Um . . . maybe . . . well, not really."

"So, like obviously, Tony's not the one you're in love with." Lisa Marie was barreling ahead with all her questions. "So who is it?"

Heather giggled and shook her head. “Details some other time,” she promised. “I’m new at this. Okay?”

“Okay,” Lisa Marie agreed. “Definitely on your timetable. But if it were a guy, you’d tell us now, so this shouldn’t be any different.”

“Yeah,” Heather said, smiling at that idea as if it made her happy. “I’ll tell you soon.”

Marianna reached across the table and gave Heather a hug. “I’m so glad you told us at all,” she said. “It’s like, you’re the same person you always were, but now we know you so much better. I love that.”

Heather blushed, maybe for the first time in her life. How interesting, Marianna thought, amazed to see a new vulnerable side to Heather. But then, she couldn’t expect her friends to stay exactly the same forever. They were all going to change . . . that’s what leaving high school was all about.

Marianna gazed out through the greasy window of the Pancake House and watched the cars go by. All those people running errands, going about their ordinary lives, shopping, buying gas, wiping slobber off their babies.

None of them knew what she and her friends had been through the night before.

“Doesn’t this feel like the final scene in a movie?” Marianna said. “The whole thing has such a morning-after vibe.”

“Yeah,” Lisa Marie said. “Or maybe the beginning of one.”

“Definitely,” Heather agreed. “It feels more like the beginning to me.”

Marianna thought about how she was going to go home and tell her dad to get off her case. And then live her life the way she wanted to from now on.

"Right," she said. "It is the opening scene. And it's an epic. Who knows how or when it will end?"

The Rules of Prom Night

#1: Never break up with your boyfriend right before the prom—unless you have a backup.

#2: Never buy the same dress as any other girl in your school.

#3: Never forget that the *real* fun begins at the after-party.

Best friends Lisa Marie, Marianna, and Heather are totally psyched. Senior Prom—the night where anything goes, and everything changes—is just two months away, and already, things are starting to get wild. Who could have thought that Lisa Marie would suddenly find herself single and juggling way too many boys? Or that Marianna' with her super-hot crush, Luke, would actually come true, by her super-strict father? And then there's Heather, who's secret of them all…

The sexiest moments, the wildest parties, the most unexpe table surprises—it all happens on Prom Night.

YOUNG ADULT
www.penguin.com

$9.99 U.S.
$12.50 CAN

ISBN 0-425-21179-7